## THE PAST WAS DEAD—AND THE PRESENT WAS A NIGHTMARE

Logan had fought years to destroy the dictators, but he wasn't free. He was still an outlaw in a ravaged land of killers, slave-traders, rapists and psychotic children. All he could do was keep running from the future . . .

# LOGAN'S WORLD

The Mind-Searing New Novel by

**William F. Nolan**

Acclaimed coauthor of the nationwide sensation

LOGAN'S RUN

# LOGAN'S WORLD

William F. Nolan

LOGAN'S WORLD

*A Bantam Book / December 1977*



ISBN 0-553-11418-2

*Published simultaneously in the United States and Canada*

---

*Bantam Books are published by Bantam Books, Inc. Its trademark, consisting of the words "Bantam Books" and the portrayal of a bantam, is registered in the United States Patent Office and in other countries. Marca Registrada. Bantam Books, Inc., 666 Fifth Avenue, New York, New York 10019.*

---

PRINTED IN THE UNITED STATES OF AMERICA

TO ALL THE WILD FRIENDS
I RAN WITH IN SCIENCE FICTION . . .

To *Forrest Ackerman*
To *Ray Bradbury*
To *Dennis Etchison*
To *Charles E. Fritch*
To *Ron Goulart*
To *George Clayton Johnson*
To *Richard Matheson*
To *Chad Oliver*
To *Ray Russell*
To *Robert Sheckley*
To *Jerry Sohl*
To *Wilson Tucker*

. . . AND TO THE MEMORY
OF THOSE NO LONGER RUNNING:

To *Charles Beaumont*
To *Anthony Boucher*
To *Frederic Brown*
To *Cleve Cartmill*
To *Rod Serling*

". . . the world as it stands is no illusion, no phantasm, no evil dream of a night; we wake up to it again for ever and ever; we can neither forget it nor deny it nor dispense with it."

—HENRY JAMES

"Sandman, Sandman,
leave my door.
Don't come back here
any more . . ."

—Fragment of a child's verse, circa 2116

# ARGOS

Argos died twice.

Beyond the 21st century, when the angry young had taken control of Earth, and space travel had been aborted, she was left to die in orbit, dwarfed by a silent Mars, her mute sun mirrors capturing energy without purpose, her womb-hub empty of life—an immense, spoked wheel turning in endless black.

Until the runners found her.

The man called Ballard knew about Argos, knew that she could provide shelter to those who fled the Sandmen and sought Sanctuary. He helped organize the lifeships that fired up from Cape Steinbeck carrying the vital stuffs of existence—hydrogen, nitrogen, carbon—to feed the arteries of the great wheel in the sterile frontier darkness beyond Earth. And, with each silver ship, eager runners arrived on Argos, free from the Sandman's Gun, to spawn fresh life in this new sea of space.

Children were born who would never know Earth. A hospital was built; fields of wheat, corn and rice were cultivated; a school was established—and fruit trees bloomed under a ribbed-glass sky.

At staggered intervals, as Ballard perfected his Sanctuary Line, more ships arrived, swelling the colony's population to more than three thousand men, women and children.

Then the lifeships stopped coming.

As a full year passed without supplies, fear began to permeate the colony. Argos was not self-sufficient; she could not survive without the stuffs of Earth.

Two years without ships.

Three. Then four.

Medical supplies were exhausted. Plague and death ran the wheel. The colony dwindled—to a thousand . . . to five hundred . . . to a hundred . . . to a handful of steel-tough runners and their families.

Logan and Jessica were among them, ten-year veterans of Argos—the legendary ex-Sandman and the woman who'd shared his desperate run for Sanctuary. They had a son now: Jaq, born on the wheel eight years ago, with the strength of his father in his pale green eyes, his mother's grace in movement, a boy who thrived on Earth history, who listened, entranced, to Logan's dark tales of a computerized world. To Jaq, the man named Ballard was a god . . .

Six years without ships.

Crisis time. The fields sere and withered. Water at a minimum. Food running out.

And one small lifeship to take them back.

Only a dozen could undertake the voyage. Lots were drawn, the final twelve chosen, the ship prepared.

On board with nine others: Logan, Jessica and Jaq.

Fireup! Away . . . away.

Away.

Behind them, in the cool depths of uncaring space, Argos began her second death.

In Old Washington, Logan discovered why the ships had stopped coming. Sandmen had penetrated and smashed the Sanctuary Line at Cape Steinbeck. Just one step ahead of them, Ballard escaped to Crazy Horse Mountain in the Dakotas, to the Thinker. There, in a final gesture of rebellion against the system, he had sacrificed himself to destroy the vast computer-complex—bringing the cities down with it. Mazecars froze on their tracks; beltways were stilled; the time crystals in the hand of each citizen no longer ticked away human life.

The power of the Sandman was broken.

Citizens poured out of the tumbled, lifeless cities into the sudden reality of a raw world. The City People, young, pampered, given every luxury by their computerized life-system, had now become the Wilderness People, bewildered and cast adrift in a harsh new environment.

For them, the illusion of freedom had turned to the reality of nightmare.

# RUN!

Logan was running.

No longer the hunter, he was the hunted. Black on black: his charcoal-dark uniform blending into night, feet stabbing the earth as he ran, dry-mouthed, for life.

The men of Deep Sleep were close behind him, relentless, kill-trained State assassins who terminated runners with the cold dispatch of the Thinker itself. Sandmen who hated him for what he'd done to them. (*"A Sandman doesn't run, Logan! He accepts Sleep proudly. You've betrayed the system, made fools of us all—and we'll homer you down for it, Logan!"*

*Homer!* It could follow him anywhere, that singing charge of pain and death, seeking the heat of his body as a bee seeks pollen, leaping and twisting as he leaped and twisted through the night spaces of the city.

Yet, they had not fired. They were savoring the hunt, tasting it like a fine wine, moving in tireless oiled motion behind him, knowing he could not outrun them or the glowing death they carried at their belts.

Why is the runner always weak, exhausted, fighting to stay afoot—while his hunters are calm, easy-breathing, unruffled? Is it fear which quakes his bones, trip-hammers his heart; the fear of impossible odds, fear of the homer's ultimate pain?

Logan feared. He was brave, resolute, superbly-conditioned, and had faced the possibility of death in many forms, but now he feared. When a homer leaves the barrel of a Sandman's Gun there is no way to deflect it from its deadly course. It finds you, hits you, rips and unravels you in a wash of searing, nerve-tortured pain. Any man would fear such a death . . .

Logan circled up through the mile-high complex, a frenzied insect caught in a maze of steel-and-metal. He was weaponless; the Gun had been lost to him a million years ago somewhere in the vastness of the city. A million-year run! His mouth gaped in pained laughter. Had he *really* been running that long? No wonder, then, that exhaustion burned fire-hot in his chest, that the world rippled in and out of focus, that his legs were loose and stupid under him, betraying his body, refusing to obey the hard command: *run . . . run . . . run!*

Run!

Logan fell.

"You all right?" Voice, filtering down to him. Hand, reaching for him. "Up you come now, Sandman. Easy does it."

Logan swayed, holding fast to the shoulder of a reed-thin citizen, blinked at him, held out his right palm.

"Your flower's blacked, has it? Then you're a runner!" The voice turned icy. "A stinking runner!"

A fist smashed into Logan's face. He lurched back, blood threading his mouth.

"Here he is! *Here!*" The man was shouting, telling the Sandmen where to find Logan. He swung dizzily away, into a snake-twist of corridor darkness.

Another lift up. A riser to the next quad level. Then, in a stagger of steps, and a cool rush of night air, through an irised exit onto the roof of the mile-high complex.

Logan's run was over. He had climbed to the summit of this metal mountain.

Around him, on all sides, the city spread pulsing, sensuous wings of light. Far below, the multicolored shimmer of Arcade devoured darkness with tongues of crystal fire.

Measured voices on the quad level directly beneath him. Sharp commands. The Sandmen were only seconds away. Logan spun toward the roof door.

Jessica was there.

Her hair glimmered like spun copper, the lights of the city caught in its soft strands. Her face was carved ivory against the night. She was beautiful.

"You need help," she said.

"No one can help me now," he told her. "Not even you."

She rippled and changed. And Jaq was there in her place.

"They're going to kill me," the boy said.

"Not you!" cried Logan. "You're *young*. Your crystal's *blue!*"

"I have no crystal." And Jaq held up his right palm. It was clear.

Logan started toward his son, wanting him to understand everything, wanting to tell him he was sorry he had ever been a Sandman, ever hunted and killed runners like himself, ever used the Gun . . .

But the Deep Sleep men were there, on the roof, weapons out and aimed at his son.

At Jaq!

The boy backed away from them, fear rising like smoke in the pale green of his eyes.

"It's *me* you want!" shouted Logan.

They ignored him, closing on Jaq in a tightening circle. The boy was at the roof's edge; he could retreat no further.

Hands fisted, Logan threw himself at the Sandmen. A backhanded blow from the barrel of a Gun stunned him, dumped him to the roof. He raised his head to scream.

Too late. Too late for everything.

They'd forced Jaq over the edge—and the boy fell in soundless, dream-spinning slow motion, doll-like, down . . . down . . . down . . . into the flame-sharp lights of Arcade.

The Sandmen swung their rifled eyes to Logan.

"Homer him," said their leader, softly.

And the charge leapt from a Gun, sang in a hot yellow arc toward Logan. Who stood to meet it.

Astonishing pain. A ripped dazzle of seared nerves as Logan collapsed in upon himself, fingers clawing air. His body exploded, flared out in ribbons of shocked flesh, into a thousand separate units of anguish. He was only pain and agony and sundered bone . . .

He was awake.

"You all right?"

Logan flinched back from the citizen's question.

Not not *his* question, not his voice. Jessica's.

She was touching him with warm, gentle hands, smoothing away the nightmare.

"The Sandmen," said Logan, staring up at her, his face flushed and sweating. "They killed Jaq."

"There's no more killing. The cities are dead, Logan. The system is dead. When will you *believe* that?"

"I believe it," he said.

"Then why do you keep having these dreams?"

He shook his head. "I don't know . . ." He looked at her. "This dream was different. In all the others, I was the only one they hunted. In this one, *Jaq* died."

"I wish you could stop having them."

"I'm worried about Jaq. How is he?"

"A little better today, I think. But he's still—"

"He's not better," said Logan flatly, rising from the

bed to slip on a velvrobe. "And he's never *going* to be until I do what Jonath told me to do." A moment of silence. "I'm going to Stoneham."

"He'll . . . want to see you before you go."

Logan nodded.

He walked through the sagging wooden house to his son's room. The mammoth three-story Colonial mansion facing the banks of the Potomac floated like a landbound ship on acres of green lawn, now gone to seed and wild growth. In its day it had served the elite of Washington; its vaulted, high-ceilinged rooms and wide hallways had echoed to week-long parties and lavish state dinners. Now it was a time-eroded relic to an unremembered past.

As he moved toward his son's room Logan thought again of the irony in this situation: Jaq had been one of the strongest boys on Argos, impervious even to the plague and sickness which had devastated the colony. Yet now, within a dozen sunsets of their return to Earth, the boy had fallen victim to an illness which spread fever through his young body, which softened bones and thinned muscles, leaving him weak and shaking, unable to function.

Logan had gone to Jonath who, at twenty-seven, was the oldest of the new breed of Wilderness People, serving as their leader in this rugged world beyond the womb cities.

"What is it, what's *wrong* with him?" Logan had asked.

"Earth is what's wrong with him," said Jonath. "Your boy has no immunity to protect him from a virus which our adult bodies would instantly reject. I would say he has contracted a form of viral pneumonia, an infant's disease."

"How do I cure it?"

"You'll need Sterozine. A nursery medroom would carry it, but the primary nurseries are all inside the cities and impossible to reach."

"Why impossible?"

"When the cities fell, the Scavengers took over. Ex-cubs . . . gypsies . . . looters . . . They run in packs. No one goes in or out. The People need food and supplies from the cities, but the Scavengers are in total control. You'd never reach a primary nursery alive, and even if you did they'd never let you leave. They carry Fusers, and burn down anyone who penetrates inner-city territory."

"There are secondary nurseries . . . Sunrise . . . Stoneham . . ."

"Yes," said Jonath. "In your place, I'd try them. But their med supplies may have already been stripped."

"It's a chance," Logan had said. "If Jaq's not better by tomorrow, I'll try Stoneham."

Jonath nodded. ". . . a chance."

"He may not *need* the drug," Logan had told him. "Jess thinks that she can pull him through this. I hate leaving them alone." He sighed. "Couldn't you be mistaken?"

"Easily," said Jonath. "I'm only guessing. We'd need a med machine to be certain. Without a full diag there's no way to be sure, but all the symptoms . . ."

The symptoms: weakness, fever, flushed features, twitching muscles . . . They were all in evidence as Logan looked down at his son. He leaned closer, touched the boy's fevered cheek.

Jaq's eyes fluttered open. He smiled, a pained stretching-back of his pale lips.

"I'm going to find something that will make you well," said Logan. "You'll be *strong* again. Soon."

"I—can't be alone." A note of panic.

"You won't be. Jess will stay with you until I'm back."

"I hate being sick," Jaq mumbled softly. Again the pained smile. "But I love *you*, Logan!"

Strange, this business of loving. Sandmen never loved. Logan had grown up believing that love was a useless emotion shared by cowards, by runners who refused to face their responsibilities to the system. He'd heard them say they loved one another, before he'd Gunned them. He'd terminated them with the word still on their lips. And felt contempt.

Did you "love" in a glasshouse? Sex wasn't love. Did you "love" a pairmate?

When you were weak and small and needed it, the Loveroom gave it to you (*Mother loves you . . . loves you . . . loves you . . .*) but, until Jessica, he hadn't thought he'd ever share it. Not Logan 3, a master of the Gun, a hunter of weaklings and cowards and misfits. Now, miracle of miracles, he had *two* human beings to love and who loved him: his wife and his son. Husband . . . wife . . . son. Old labels, worn by those who had rejected the system and gone back to ancient customs. Ugly, how the Thinker had twisted everything, distorted emotion, crippled and warped. Jaq had been right about Ballard: he *was* a god. He'd killed the Thinker . . .

Jess walked out to the paravane with him. Logan wore a dark blue citizen's tunic, open at the neck, vested in leather.

"You'll be back before dark?"

"Yes," he said, climbing into the control pod, activating the gyroblades, rear blade first, then overhead. The blades shivered into motion, began revolving in a vibrating blur, feeding power into the small craft.

They were on a section of high grass facing the Potomac, and the afternoon sun flashed fire-colors off the wind-sculptured rocks scattered along the dry riverbed. Before the Little War, before climactic changes had blocked off the Potomac, it had flowed richly with water. Must have been beautiful then, thought Logan, this spot facing the river. So *much* had changed . . .

"He's sleeping now," Jess said, her voice keyed to the rising hum of the blades. "He'll be all right until you get back."

Logan leaned out to kiss her.

She was crying.

Afraid I won't find the drug, Logan told himself. Afraid I'll be too late. *But I'll find it! Jess, I'll find it!*

Trim level: corrected. Gyro controls: stable. Power curve: normal. Logan engaged vertical thrust—and the paravane soared gracefully upward, quickly attained cruising altitude, then tipped westward in a singing rush of blades.

Toward Stoneham.

## STONEHAM

Each major city area had its secondary nurseries, its Stoneham and Sunrise units; Logan had terminated a female runner once, near Stoneham, in the Angeles Complex. (*"Please don't hurt me, Sandman! I want to live. I'm only twenty-one . . . that isn't really old . . . can't you . . ."*) And the homer leaving the Gun. And the girl scrabbling along the high fence, the horror in her eyes. And the homer—

*Stop it!*

Logan shut down the memory.

The primary nurseries were much larger, and handled most of the city infants; these outside units were designed to take up the overflow, but were complete in themselves. There was more than a good chance he'd find Sterozine at a secondary unit.

Adults had no use for the drug. It would fetch nothing on the Market, and would be a useless item to outland looters.

A good chance . . .

Had his mission been less critical Logan would have enjoyed the flight to Stoneham. The sky was a serene blue, the green land rich and rolling beneath him—and the paravane was sound and responsive, thanks to his work on it over the past seven days since he and Jess had found the machine, abandoned outside the city-ruins. It had been damaged in the city's fall, had fluttered down, broken-bladed, to kill its pilot. Logan's mechanical skills, honed in his years on Argos, had quickly restored it to perfect working order.

Fuel wasn't a problem, since the craft's solar-charged unit would provide unlimited range, and Logan was fully confident that he would encounter no malfunction in flight.

But thoughts of Jaq kept darkening his mind, canceling out the natural joys of soaring above the land . . .

Then he sighted the heavy mass of bulked gray stone rising from a hill to his left. Stoneham.

Logan cut primepower on the aft blade, swinging the paravane at a sharp arc downward and to the left, clearing the nursery's microwire fence. He gentled the craft to a smooth touchdown in the central court area, killed the blades, slid free of the controls.

Incredible silence. His landing had set off no alarm systems; no automated guards rushed toward him; no robotic defense devices were activated. He remembered running with Jess from just such a nursery as this in the Dakotas—through a chaos of sirens and bells—fighting his way free of machines and closing gates and menacing robots.

This time, nothing. He was free to walk inside.

Yet Logan felt uneasy, prowling the long, dust-silent corridors, searching for the Medroom. He'd hated growing up in this sterile environment, denied all outside human contact for the first seven years of his life. His talk puppet had been his only real friend (*"I'll never forget you, Loge . . . never forget you!"*) and his dream of becoming a Sandman had sustained him. The *pride* he'd felt in the word in those days! *Sandman!* The psyc machines had brainwashed him thoroughly from birth. If it had not been for Jess . . .

Suddenly an old memory clicked into place for him: Playroom . . . Deliveryroom . . . Cribroom . . . Medroom. That was the way Autogoverness had taken him whenever he got sick, rolling along the hall with him, clucking at him in her soulless metal voice, telling him he'd soon feel fine, just fine.

Logan found the Playroom, entered—and instantly fell into a defensive crouch. Something was *alive* inside the room, flickering at him, away from him, at him again.

Logan smiled. In entering, he'd simply dislodged one of the vibroballs, and it was dancing its self-energized puzzle pattern from ceiling to floor. He reached out, caught and boxed it, moved quickly on.

The Deliveryroom. Logan stared with fresh awe at the large Hourglass dominating the chamber; it had *always* fascinated him. Inside: the glittering time crystals ready for implant in the palm of each new infant brought to Nursery. Logan closed his right fist around his own dead crystal, remembering the sick shock which had run through his body when his timeflower had begun to blink red-black . . . red-black . . . red-black . . . telling him he had just twenty-four hours before Last-day.

Damn the Thinker and the horrors it had inflicted!

He turned to enter the Cribroom.

Logan was used to death; he'd dispatched it to others, had seen his friends die in Sleepshops, had faced massed death on Argos—but what he found here, in this dank, silent room, stunned him.

In each of the small, bullet-shaped cribs lining the four walls lay a tiny skeleton. Here were the delicate bones of a hundred babies who had died when the

Thinker died, oxygen cut off, vital fluids denied them. Their small white skulls mocked Logan with dark, eyeless sockets as he moved past them toward the med supplies.

He found another corpse in the Medroom. An Autogoverness lay on her side, her dozen jointed arms frozen, rust already gathering in thin, red lines along her seams. In her metal fingers she grasped vials and bottles. Apparently she'd gone for the medicine in a vain effort to revive the dying infants, unaware of the fact that nothing she could do would save them. Logan stepped over her, tense and nervous.

Would he find Sterozine here?

Hurriedly, he ripped open panels, pored over shelved items, discarding, sifting, searching . . . At least the Medroom had not been stripped. If a secondary nursery carried Sterozine a supply should *be* here.

Teromitcone . . . Hydrafane . . . Ritlan-C . . . Eztem-F . . .

But no Sterozine.

Only a primary nursery carried the drug Jaq needed.

Logan knew he had no choice now.

He would face the Scavengers.

# THIRTEEN

"Kill him."

"But why?'

"He's unlucky for us."

"Luck has no foundation as a realistic belief concept."

Lucrezia didn't argue. They were thirteen and the new rider *made* them thirteen, which was unlucky. She would do it herself if Prince would not.

It was newly-dark—the night prior to Logan's death dream—and they had camped in the dry bed of a ravine, ringing a fire that painted their rouged faces in flickering shades of red and orange.

Lucrezia reached into the saddle of her jetcycle, took out a soft leather scabbard lined in blue velvet, removed a neddle-thin jeweled dagger from the scabbard, and returned to the circle of outlanders.

The thirteenth rider, thin and shag-haired, sat cross-legged at the fire. He was tearing at the leg of the hyena they'd cooked for supper, tossing aside bones as he cleared them of flesh. Totally engrossed in filling his lean stomach after a long fast, he ignored Lucrezia as she moved up behind him.

"You're unlucky for us," she said quietly, and drove the thin silver blade into the back of his neck, at the upper tip of the spinal column.

He died instantly, spilling loosely sideways into the dirt. His eyes remained open, staring at the fire he could no longer see. The others looked at his sprawled body, then at Lucrezia.

"I should have poisoned him," she said to them, a white-toothed smile making her face radiant in the firelight. "That would have been more appropriate. And *far* more romantic."

Now they were twelve again, outlanders from the New York Complex, nine males and two other females, dressed the way Lucrezia had taught them to dress: in plumed hats, in velvets, with lace at their throats, heavy gold chains strung at their necks—with jeweled swords and Florentine daggers on the saddles of their jetcycs. When the New York Complex fell they'd raided an ancient museum, finding these clothes and the Borgia history that went with them. As their leader, Anan 9 dubbed herself Lucrezia, and named her pairmate Prince, in honor of Cesare, most notorious of the Borgia males.

Now Prince said, "I'm bored. We need to claim

again." Playfully he swung his burnweapon toward a dark stand of thick brush fronting the bank, thumbed the charge. The brush ignited in a gout of flame, charred away to dead ash.

"Tomorrow," said Lucrezia, "we'll ride the Potomac."

## DAKK

It was late afternoon when Logan reached the city.

He brought the paravane down a half-mile short of the ruins. No use alerting anyone this early; they'd know about him soon enough. He used loose branches to screen the craft; if he got out he'd need it again.

If he got out.

What are your chances? Maybe fifty-fifty. Wrong! Ninety-ten against. You're unarmed, alone, invading *their* territory. All right, ninety-ten. But unless I get the Sterozine, Jaq has *no* chance.

Logan entered the heart of the Complex through one of the abandoned maze tunnels, moving with Sandman's stealth, making certain his feet did not trample the dead brush littering the alum flooring. A snapped twig would echo like a nitro shot in here.

The tunnel's arching mirror-surface was dulled by dust; afternoon sun bled through finger-thin cracks in the overhead metal. A shadowy bulk loomed ahead of Logan, half filling the tunnel: a dead mazecar, overturned like a giant metal insect in the silent gloom, its yellowed tonneau split and shattered, controls red with six years' rust. It was occupied. By two skeletons.

Logan stepped around them. After the infants in Nursery, he experienced no shock reaction whatever to the remains of these two dead citizens. He knew he would see many more inside the city—and if the Scavengers had their way, his own skeleton would join the others.

He came out of the tunnel onto a maze platform: Level Six, Quadrant K, Platform J-211. Industrial Sector. Which meant he could cut through Sandman Headquarters and take a slidechute to Arcade. The nearest primary nursery was just beyond that point. He'd have to risk the chute; if he tried to walk it they'd spot him for sure.

Now Logan entered the city proper, vast and deserted in the fading rays of the late-afternoon sun. No, not deserted. The Scavengers were here, and would instantly reveal their presence if he miscalculated. But if he moved shadow-quiet to his destination, senses attuned to the slighest danger, he *might* just make it.

Logan was amazed at how quickly wilderness was claiming the city. Already, in just half a dozen years, vines and creepers were choking the beltways, and rank grass thrust up in profusion between cracked pavements. The city would soon be jungle, like Old Washington itself.

The towering gray monolith of DS Headquarters disturbed Logan, symbolizing all too forcefully what he had been and done in the service of the Thinker. He'd been one of the DS elite, with a truly impressive record of kills. No runner escaped his Gun. How many human beings had he proudly Gunned in his years of city service—brave, rational citizens who desperately wanted to live beyond their twenty-first birthdays?

Logan shut down the memories; it was useless to feel guilt for his past. Just be glad that it's over, that the killing is done and that you're back in the city on a mission to *save* a life, not to take one.

He passed through the dead brain-center of the report room, once alive with flashing computer readouts and humming alert boards. Runners had no chance against a system such as this, yet the instinct for survival kept them going—and some, a scattered few, actually made it to Sanctuary. Thanks to Ballard—and Jessica—Logan had been one of those few.

He stopped now at the Gunroom, impulsively reached out to pick up a small silver cylinder. He weighed it in his hand. Ammopac. Notched into its six chambers: tangler, ripper, needler, nitro, vapor—and homer. Logan slipped the cylinder into his tunic. Not that he'd ever use these deadly charges again, but this would satisfy the consuming curiosity of Jaq. On Argos, the boy had often questioned him about the Gunpac. Now he could see one for himself. A token of the city.

The slidechute would be tricky. It was safe enough, with its antigrav force unaffected by computer breakdown; the chute would still carry him to the Arcade area quickly and efficiently, but he must be very careful not to bump the narrow sides with foot or elbow. As in a maze tunnel, the smallest sound would be greatly amplified.

Logan was careful. The sensation of gently floating downward was akin to freefall in the ships: pleasant but somewhat unsettling.

On the lower Arcade Level he checked the outer terrain before stepping free of the chute. Clear. Silent. No movement.

Maybe Jonath had exaggerated the number of Scavengers in the city, or perhaps they'd abandoned this one entirely, gone on to richer pickings. Certainly he could detect no sign of them.

But Logan kept his senses at hyper-alert status; he could not afford to relax.

A shadow within shadows, he moved through Arcade.

The outlanders rode the Potomac. They'd enjoyed themselves earlier in the day with a Wilderness group near the Library of Congress, forcing the men to watch while the nine Borgia males stripped and assaulted the Wilderness females. It had just been high-spirited fun until one of the males broke free to a jetcycle, jump-started the machine, and tried to run down three of the Borgias. The jetcyc belonged to Prince, and Lucrezia could sympathize with her pairmate's anger over the theft—and had helped garrote the rogue with a silken belt taken from a Wilderness girl.

The fellow had kicked like a fish, and it had all been most amusing once he'd been caught and dealt with. But Prince's machine had been badly damaged when it had struck a banyan root and overturned. That meant they were short a cycle, and Prince had to double-ride behind Ariosto.

Which explained his foul mood on the Potomac run.

The riverbed was treacherous with boulders and silt-hidden logs, but the Borgia riders enjoyed the risk, weaving their machines around each obstacle with obvious delight, challenging one another in brief, brutal contests of speed and agility.

Prince took no pleasure in any of this; he was saddlesore, anxious to dismount.

"Camptime!" he yelled. And, one by one, the riders cut power, the whine of their jets keening down to silence. Prince eased himself stiffly to the ground as Lucrezia, her face tight with fury, roared up to him. She'd been leading the riders and was the last to note that the others had stopped.

"You pisswhelp!" she screamed, and struck Prince across the face with a short leather riding crop, splitting his skin. "Nobody calls camptime but the leader, and *I* lead here!"

Prince whined, nursing his wound. "I'm hungry. My bones ache from riding backsaddle. There's no reason not to camp."

"No reason except I say we don't," said Lucrezia. She raised an imperial hand to the others. "Riders up!"

The outlanders remounted their machines, jump-fired them to life again.

"You coming—or staying?" the leader asked Prince.

He looked defeated as he moved toward Ariosto's machine.

Jaq had slept all afternoon and was awake when his mother came to bring him water. His throat was dry all the time now, and the water didn't help much—but Jess told him he'd be feeling a lot better just as soon as Logan got back with the medicine.

"Do Earth people still die?" he asked her.

Jess smiled. "Of course. Everyone dies sometime. It's just that there are no Sandmen any more to force you to die before your normal time."

"What's my normal time?"

"I don't know that, Jaq." She smiled again, but there was a shade of concern behind her eyes. "Maybe you'll live to be a hundred. In old, old times some people lived that long."

"On Argos everyone died quickly."

"That's because they were sick with the plague and had no medicine to cure them. You'll be cured when your father brings you the proper medicine." She looked at him intently, stroked his hair with tentative fingers. "Are you worried about dying?"

"No," said Jaq. "Just about living and being sick. I hate being sick."

"Drink your water and try to sleep some more. Until Logan gets back."

"I'll try," said Jaq. "But I don't think I can sleep until he does. I hope he hurries."

Jessica looked out the window, at the dry Potomac. "I hope so, too," she said softly.

She didn't say what she was thinking—that she felt totally vulnerable without Logan, totally *alone*.

For no reason at all, a sense of dread was building within her.

Logan had never seen Arcade like this: empty, silent, colorless. Always the Arcade sector of each city pulsed with crowds—citizens eager for sensual delights, pouring through these vast pleasure centers in a ceaseless stream, seeking bizarre sensations, new thrills (*"Come in, citizen, and bathe in living flame!"*) . . . But now the firegalleries, the Re-Live parlors, glasshouses and hallucimills were stark and lifeless.

Logan moved quickly past a gutted firegallery, striped in shadow and smelling of dead charcoal. He angled through a Re-Live parlor, passing tiers of deadmetal lifedrawers, moved across a stilled beltway fronting a dust-glazed New You and a shattered glasshouse (*Pleasure . . . Satisfaction . . . Rare Delights . . .*) to his goal.

Nursery.

Logan drew in a long, cautious breath, expelled the air slowly from his lungs. He was here at last.

He checked the interior. No one inside.

Slipping past the long lines of coffin-cribs, each holding its tiny white skeleton, he moved swiftly for the medshelves.

They'd been stripped.

In frustration, Logan slammed his fist against the wall. And realized, in the same instant, that he had advertised his presence in the city.

If they were still here.

If they had heard the sound.

Then Logan felt a surge of hope. Despite the fact that the med supplies had been stripped, the drug he wanted *could* have been left behind, since it had no value to Scavengers. He began searching—prying open panels, sifting through rusting tubes, boxes, hexagonal containers.

Until he found it. An entire case of it: *Sterozine X-cc 6466*, ranked in red metaloid tubes. Untouched.

He didn't need much; one canister would be more than enough to cure Jaq. Logan selected one, made sure there were no splits in the metaloid casing, then slipped it into his tunic next to the Gun cylinder.

A faint, scraping sound behind him. Logan was motionless. An animal? Cat, maybe. Or . . .

He turned.

The Scavengers were there.

The sun was almost down when Lucrezia saw the mansion. She raised a hand to alert the other riders, swinging her jetcyc around in a spume of gravel to face the hill. At its tip, riding the waves of high grass, the mansion rose up dark against the sky, imposing and grand to behold.

Lucrezia smiled. A smile of possession.

The Potomac had produced a prize.

## CAPTURE

Dakk studied the invader.

Tall. Well-muscled. A hardness in the eyes. Strong arms. He could be dangerous. There was something about his face, something familiar . . .

The others were watching Dakk, waiting for the signal. Killing an invader was a rare treat. You didn't get many in the cities anymore. At first, a lot of them had come in, looking for things they needed, but when they didn't ever come out again the word spread fast: keep clear of the Scavengers.

But now they had a fresh one, and they'd have a fine time with him once Dakk gave the signal. A really fine time.

"How did you get here?" Dakk asked the invader. "We didn't see you, didn't hear you?"

"Does it matter?" said Logan.

"You better answer all my questions . . . We run the city now."

"You don't run it—you feed off its corpse!"

Dakk smiled thinly. "Look, I'm very interested. You're the first one who's gotten this far in without us seeing him. I'd like to know how you did it."

"I have a son," said Logan. "He's eight, and dying. He needs Sterozine. The drug's no good to you. No one uses it. No one trades for it. But, right now, it can save my son's life. I don't want anything else from you or from the city. You can keep it all. Just let me go."

As he talked, Logan knew it was useless, that his words were empty and meaningless to a group of amoral savages—but, for Jaq's sake, he had to try.

"Aren't you afraid of us?" asked Dakk quietly. "Tell us you're afraid."

"I'm afraid of you," said Logan.

"That's good to know." Dakk turned to the others and smiled broadly. "Shall we let him go?"

They smiled back at him, a wolf pack numbering more than twenty, all young, all lean and feral and dressed to fit their name—in scavenged clothing plucked at random from the cities. Dakk was typical: he wore the boots of a Sandman, the gleaming, scaled bodysuit of a glassdancer; the sash around his head, keeping long, blond, uncut hair from his eyes, had belonged to a Wilderness girl he'd trapped and killed in Arcade. She'd been looking for her brother, who'd been trapped and killed by another pack.

Now Dakk regarded Logan with mounting interest. This invader was strong and healthy; he should provide good sport for them.

"All right, you can go," said Dakk with a shrug. "But only if you tell me how you got this far. It's something I'd really like to know."

"I came in through a maze tunnel at Level Six," Logan told him. "Used a slidechute from DS to Arcade, kept to shadows, walked soft. Satisfied?"

"You're good—very good," nodded Dakk. "The others who came in, they knocked over things, made a lot of noise. You *deserve* to go." He smiled again, spreading his hands in an open gesture. "So go."

Logan knew it was a trick. They'd never let an invader leave the city alive. It was to be a game with them, running him down before he could find a way out. They were the sharks, and it was *their* sea. If this pack didn't catch him, another pack would—since he'd have no time for caution, no chance to run on his own terms. But he'd known the odds before coming into the city. Now he'd live—or die—with them.

So Logan ran.

And Dakk, smiling, watched him go.

"It's almost dark, and Logan isn't back."

"Go to sleep, Jaq."

"You keep saying that. But I can't, Jessica, I *told* you I can't."

"He'll come soon, I know."

They were after him already, didn't want to lose him to another pack. But Logan had used his ten-second head start to good advantage. Normally, an invader would be expected to go for the nearest direct route leading outside—but Logan circled, came in *behind* the nursery, entered the structure again, doubling back on a reverse line.

Which bought him some time.

He thought of finding a safe spot and settling in until morning. But that was no good. By then every pack in the city would be looking for him, and with full light to trap him by. No, he'd have to get out *now*, the best way he could.

Sleepshop! Logan smiled to himself. Each shop had its own unique exit—a chute which led directly to the atomic burnbins at the bottom level of the city. When a citizen was put to sleep in a shop his effects were placed in a wall canister, bearing his name and number; then his corpse was chuted for burndown. The furnaces were dead now, and safe for Logan. Once there, he could slip easily out of the city-complex.

Where was the nearest Sleepshop? None in Arcade; too depressing for joy-bent citizens. But since this nursery was just beyond Arcade a shop should be close.

Logan found one, moving like a drift of smoke along the inner walkways, avoiding the belts, keeping alert for Scavengers. He reached the shop, ducked quickly inside.

He paused to listen—and could hear the pack, several quads away, frustratedly hunting him.

Dakk was angry. Mainly at himself. He had no business giving this invader a ten-second head start. The fellow was clever, or he never would have been able to reach Nursery. I should have kept him in sight all the way, Dakk told himself. You don't gamble with the smart ones; they can fox you. If we lose him for good Ritter might make his bid for control of the pack. He's been itching to take my place. They might even . . .

Dakk turned his thoughts away from what the pack might do to him if this invader actually escaped the city. It was his job to catch him, kill him. And he would.

" . . . not in this area," Ritter was saying to the others. He walked over to Dakk—a soft-faced, slack-jawed bully, with small pig's eyes, soft and wet. Dakk hated Ritter.

"Any ideas?" he asked Dakk. The tone was bitter, mocking.

"This one's different. He'll make for a place we wouldn't think of looking," Dakk improvised. His thoughts raced: *where, where, where?*

Ritter grinned. "And just where would that be?"

Suddenly Dakk relaxed; a wave of relief and triumph swept through him. "I think I know," he said.

Jessica saw them coming, jetting up from the Potomac. Outlanders. They'd want food, any goods of value.

She stopped onto the pillared veranda.

I can handle them, she told herself. It will be all right. When they see I have nothing they'll leave.

The cycles flamed out, into silence. Lucrezia dismounted, withdrew a longsword from her saddle, raised it. The tall blade captured the rays of dying sun, flashing.

She looked regally at Jessica. Her voice was commanding. "I, Lucrezia, daughter of Alexander the Seventh, wife of Alfonso, duke of Ferrara, sister to Cesare, duke of Valentinois, do herewith, on this day, claim thy castle, and all within it, as mine own."

She lowered the sword, a signal for the others to dismount.

Jessica found herself amused at this theatrical display of pomp. She shook her head. "You're welcome to the place—but there's nothing of value here for you to claim."

"We'll decide that for ourselves," said Lucrezia, mounting the wide wooden steps of the veranda. Prince and the others followed.

"We have some water, a small amount of food—and little else," said Jess.

Prince stopped, gave Jessica a long stare. "I want her," he said to Lucrezia.

"Then she's yours."

Jessica stepped hastily back, toward the inner hallway. Her amusement had given way to a pervasive feeling of terror.

"I'm mated," she said. "My pairman is Logan." His name put sudden strength in her voice. "We have a son."

"Ah . . ." Lucrezia nodded. "And where is he, this son of yours?"

"Inside sleeping."

"And your Logan . . . Is he inside, too?"

It was no use lying to them. They could find out the truth easily enough by searching the mansion. "He's . . . gone. To get medicine for our boy."

"How long will he be gone?" asked one of the females. She was willow-tall, with sensuous eyes. Her name was Ris. She, too, looked at Jessica with a special hunger.

"He's due back any time now," said Jessica. "If you try to harm me . . ."

Ris swayed her body close to Jessica. Her mouth was pouting. "We won't harm you. We just want to—"

Prince pushed her roughly. "She's *mine!* You heard Lucrezia." He turned to the leader. "Can I take her now?" He fondled Jessica's hair, grinning as she flinched away from his touch.

"Of course, darling," said Lucrezia. She placed the needle tip of a dagger playfully against Jessica's throat. "Though you may have to *share*. Ris seems to want her. And we must not forget Ariosto, who allowed you to share *his* mount."

"No sharing on this one! I *won't!*"

Ariosto chuckled, nodding his large head. He was square, burly-faced and viciously stupid. "You will, Prince, you will. If she says so, you will."

Lucrezia smiled, pleased at the shock and despair on Jessica's face. "We'll just have to see who takes you, won't we?"

And she kissed Jessica deeply, with an open, wet tongue.

Logan had to exert extreme muscular control in negotiating the narrow burnchute. It did not operate on antigrav, which meant he could easily lose his footing and tumble all the way down into the furnace many levels below. Exhausted when he finally reached the floor of the furnace, he staggered, bracing himself, on the way to the exit hatch.

Before he could reach out to disengage the holdrod, the hatch was jerked abruptly open from the other side.

Dakk was there, grinning at him. "We were *both* smart," he said to Logan. "You for choosing this way out—and me for figuring you would."

Logan slumped back against the metal wall of the furnace. "You've won your game," he said tightly.

"But it isn't over yet," said Ritter.

The others, clustered in a circle around the furnace, murmured agreement.

"We have a little gift for invaders," said Dakk, producing a small blue pellet from a tooled leather wrist-pouch. He handed Logan the pellet.

"Swallow it," said Baxter 2. He stood behind Ritter.

"Poison?" asked Logan.

"No," smiled Dakk. "We're not going to kill you so soon. You heard what Ritter said: the game's still on." His voice took on hardness. "Now *swallow* it."

Logan knew he had no choice.

He swallowed the pellet.

## DEATH

And Albert 6 was there, talking to him. A nice surprise for Logan.

"I love you, Loge."

Albert sat on his lap. "What'll we talk about today?"

"What we always talk about," said Logan to the small, serious-eyed figure.

"Oh, *that* again."

"But it's fun to talk about being a Sandman!"

"For you, maybe, but not for me. I can never be

one. I'm just a puppet. When you leave they'll put me away in a box."

Suddenly, Albert fell over.

"What's wrong?"

"You killed him," said Dakk. "You killed your little friend. Now you have *no* one. You're all alone."

Logan began to sweat. "I need to get out."

"You'll never get out," said Warden. "You're in Hell. And no one gets out of Hell. I'm in charge. I ought to know."

"It's a long way down," Lilith told him. "You have to be careful."

A mile-deep emptiness yawned beneath him. He didn't trust Lilith. "You don't believe I'm running, do you?"

"You're a Sandman," said Ballard. "Why should *anyone* believe a Sandman?"

Karenya 3 put her hand on his groin. She caressed him there in a slow, sensuous rhythm, arousing him to full erectness. "Lie back," she said, her lips close to his. "Just lie back and see what I can do for you."

She was nude, her perfect body bathed in gold.

And green.

And red.

And blue.

And yellow.

"I have to get to Headquarters. Francis is waiting."

"No, Francis is dead," she whispered. "Here . . . touch my breasts."

"Do as she says," Dakk told him.

Logan cupped her left breast; it was like cool marble. He lowered his mouth to it, laved it with his tongue. It tasted of honey.

Jessica groaned. "Take me, Logan, take me *now!*"

And he entered her in a long, flowing movement, filling her, his weight pressing her slim ivory back into the foam.

"It's all right," said Doyle. "She's my sister, and she loves you. I don't mind. Go right ahead."

"Thank you," said Logan—and began thrusting deeply, withdrawing, thrusting again. Until his groans matched hers, until the pressure building within could no longer be denied.

"Wild me, Sandfella!" screamed Graygirl.

And Logan cried out sharply as his seed spurted into the warm depths of her body.

"That was good, wasn't it?" asked Ritter.

"Yes," said Logan.

"Don't move," crooned Box. "Let me capture the moment, let me immortalize it." His cutting hand moved in a blur of blue ice.

Logan grabbed Francis, held him by both shoulders. "There's no use to any of it, is there?"

"What do you mean?"

"This whole rotten business. We hunt and we kill and we hunt again. Until we die or someone hunts us."

"We're the elite, Logan." Francis smiled, his thin lips drawn back tightly. "We have the best of everything . . . jewels . . . food . . . women . . ."

Whale laughed at this, his immense belly quaking. "For how long, though? Ask him *that,* Logan. For how much longer?"

And Box said, "Done!" He looked at Logan. "You may leave now."

"But where can I go?"

"That's up to you. Nobody can tell you that."

"Come with me," said Holly. "You can have a new face."

"I don't want to change," said Logan.

"Everyone changes," Holly smiled. "It's the thing to do."

"She's right," said Dakk.

"Do it!" said Rutago.

But he didn't want to lie down on the Table.

"Relax," said Doc. "Just close your eyes."

"Not permitted," said the Autogoverness. "You'll have to leave."

"Why?" asked Logan.

"I need not give reasons," she said. "I'm in total control."

"You're a machine!"

"Of course," said the Watchman. "And I'm programmed to destroy anyone who comes here. Why did *you* come here?"

"I had nowhere else to go."

The Watchman had no face, so Logan could not find a common level of communication.

"You'll be all right," said the girl in glitterskins. "But watch out for Francis. *He'll* try to kill you."

Harry 7 had the ice dagger, but Logan did not feel its chill. He felt great heat. Hazed smoke flowed and billowed around him. His lungs burned and he could not catch his breath.

"Don't fight it, citizen," warned the burning man beside him. "*Enjoy* it."

Logan looked down at his body. It was bathed in flame.

"Firegalleries are enchanting," said the girl in glitterskins. "They cleanse one completely. And you need to be cleansed, Logan."

"Of your sins," said Ballard. "Do you believe in sin, Logan?"

"No," said Logan. "It's an ancient concept created to control men's minds. Manipulation through guilt."

"I think the only sin lies in hurting others," said Chaney Moon.

"I don't hurt anyone," said Logan.

"You use the Gun," said Doyle, with bitterness. "You hunt and kill with it."

"My job. My duty."

"Absolutely correct," said Sharps.

"You twist things."

"I twist nothing," said Francis.

Logan turned to face the cubs. Whirling, dodging, ripping at him.

"I'll cut you good, Sandman!" boasted Charming Billy. "You and your runnergirl."

Jessica took Logan's arm. "He's just a boy."

"He's a cub!" protested Logan, trying to make her understand. "A savage!"

But Jess spun away into darkness.

"Wild me," said Graygirl.

"Obey me," said Autogoverness.

"Pose for me," said Box.

"Listen to me," said Ballard.

"Change for me," said Holly.

"Talk to me," said Albert.

"Trust me," said Lilith.

"Fear me," said Warden.

"Run from me," said Francis.

"Spare me," said Doyle.

"Cure me," said Jaq.

"Save me," said Jessica.

Logan put his hands against his skull and screamed. Soundlessly.

He opened his eyes.

"You had a prime lift," said Dakk.

"We like to watch," Ritter told him. "Never know what'll happen. Always interesting."

"Burn him," another Scavenger said.

Dakk nodded. "Game's over, Logan. Time to die."

"Let me," said Ritter, drawing a Fuser from his belt.

Logan braced himself against the wall of the furnace, waiting for the heatcharge.

Ritter brought up the weapon.

"Kill him," said Dakk.

"Don't!" screamed Jessica.

"Do it," Lucrezia commanded. "*Kill* him!"

And Prince fired at the boy.

Jaq took the heatcharge full in the chest, and was flung backward into the hallway.

Jessica ran to him, stared down in horror, hands to her mouth.

Lucrezia walked up to stand beside her. "He should have stayed in his room, not tried to stop us. Still . . . a sick boy is no good, of no value. We're taking you, but we couldn't take him. So let's assume he's better off the way he is."

"You . . . monster!" Jessica trembled violently, fists clenched. "You filthy, vile—"

And she clawed at Lucrezia's throat in a killing frenzy. Ariosto and two of the others pulled her away.

"Let's take her and go," said Prince. He kicked over a scrolled rosewood table in disgust. It crashed to the floor, sending a hollow echo through the mansion. "There's nothing else here."

Lucrezia rubbed at the skin of her neck, where Jessica's fingers had closed around her windpipe. "You'll regret causing me discomfort," Lucrezia said to her.

And she doubled her right fist, smashing it into Jessica's face.

Prince caught her as she fell.

"She's yours," smiled Lucrezia. "Treat her well."

"Wait!" shouted Dakk. "Don't fire!"

Ritter lowered the Fuser, looking sour. "Now what's wrong?"

Dakk walked up very close to Logan, staring at him with probing intentness. "I *thought* I'd seen him before . . ."

"I don't know you," said Logan.

"But I know *you.* When I was a cub in the Angeles Complex you came in after a runner named Doyle. But we killed him first. We cut him to pieces." Dakk turned to the others, his smile flashing. "He's Logan 3."

A murmur ran the pack. They'd all heard of him—

the only Sandman to make Sanctuary. He was already a legend.

Ritter was excited. "Let's show him to the other packs. We can kill him in front of them, make a ceremony of his death."

"No, he goes free," said Dakk flatly.

"But he's famous!" objected Ritter. "And killing him will make *us* famous."

"I said no."

"Give us a reason," said Baxter 2, who usually backed up Ritter. "A *good* reason."

Dakk turned on them, fierce-eyed. "Logan killed Charming Billy in Cathedral. If he hadn't, Billy would have killed *me*. I was a threat to him. The other cubs supported me, and Billy knew it. So . . . Logan saved my life. Now I'm saving his."

"Your reason isn't *our* reason," said Ritter tightly.

Dakk measured him coldly. "Challenge?"

A moment of silent tension between them. Then Ritter sighed, turned away.

Dakk said to Logan, "Go. The debt's paid."

Logan nodded.

"But don't ever come back," Dakk warned. "If you do, you won't leave here again. Is that understood?"

"Understood," said Logan.

And he left the city.

## GUN

The paravane had not been disturbed. Logan had some difficulty locating its exact position in the darkness, but he soon had the brush stripped away and the blades cleared.

Now he'd be able to help Jaq. The drug his son needed was safe inside his tunic, and it was a short flight back to their home on the Potomac.

Rising above the lightless mass of the city, Logan engaged full thrust—and the paravane responded smoothly. He'd been gone for most of the day, and Jess was probably worried about him, but she'd be overjoyed to learn he'd found the Sterozine. He'd been very fortunate with Dakk; by all rights he should be a dead man now. Logan had no memory of the dark-eyed leader as a cub. All the young ones blended in his mind: soot-faced, ragged, dangerous. But he remembered Charming Billy well enough. Thirteen and deadly, on Muscle, with his pride in having cut a Sandman . . .

Logan had never regretted killing him.

The house was silent as Logan approached it. Only the sound of wind in tall grass; of a nightbird, sounding its high, sweet lament.

"Jess! I'm back!"

Odd. She should have been watching for him, heard the paravane land, be out here to meet him.

*Something's wrong.*

Logan reached the veranda, stopped. The door was open.

He mounted the steps quickly, entered the hall.

And stumbled over Jaq.

Agony twisted Logan's features as he examined the body. Chest charred and ripped. Skin like cool wax. No pulse. No heartbeat.

An odor of cooked flesh in the air.

Logan let the fact sink into his mind like a heavy stone: Someone had murdered his son!

*And where was Jessica?*

He raged through the dark house, calling her name, smashing furniture in his frenzy, hurling himself from room to room, a man demented.

She was gone.

Logan threw the canister of Sterozine furiously against the steps, stumbled into the yard, fell to his knees in the wet grass, sobbing brokenly. He should never have left them alone. *Damn him!* He should have been there to defend them against—

*Against who?*

Logan raised his head. His eyes burned with a cold, killing fire. He'd find out who. Use his Sandman's training. Analyze the area. Maybe Jess was still alive.

He stood, moved to the veranda and carefully examined the gravel fronting the steps. In the marble wash of moonlight he could make out tracks, footprints . . .

"We saw them," a soft voice behind him said.

Logan pivoted to face a girl no older than seven. She wore a sunfrock trimmed in realflowers and carried a battered talkdoll. She giggled. "This is Judee 3," she said, holding up the doll. "And I'm Bet."

"*Who* did you see?" asked Logan, fighting to keep his voice level.

"The beautiful people," said Bet.

And the doll said, in a matter-of-fact voice, "They *were* lovely."

"Tell me everything about them," said Logan, crouching beside Bet, his eyes intense on hers.

"They wore pretty things. Lace and velvet. And hats with long feathers." Her voice was slow and dreamy.

And her doll said, "She's lifted. On C. That's why she's this way."

"Want one?" asked Bet, giggling sleepily. She withdrew a small capsule from her sunpocket. "Give you a prime lift. I use them all the—"

Logan knocked the drugcap from the little girl's hand, gripped her thin shoulders. "Tell me, *now,* everything you saw!"

"Judee can tell you," said the girl. "Ask *her.*"

And she giggled.

Logan slapped her. "I'm asking *you!*"

The little girl whimpered as tears brimmed her eyes. "Didn't see much . . . were leaving when we came here . . ."

"How many?"

"Don't know."

"A dozen," said the talkdoll firmly. "I counted. They rode jetcycs."

"Outlanders!" breathed Logan.

"With swords," said the doll. "And daggers."

"I feel sick," said Bet. "I'm going home now."

Logan grabbed her, spun her around to face him. "You're not going anywhere until I know *all* you know. . . . Did they have Jess?"

The little girl looked blank.

"My pairmate! Did you see them take her?"

"Yes," whimpered Bet. "They hit her and she fell and they put her on one of their cycles and rode off with her."

"Describe them!"

"I did already."

"I told you she's lifted," said the doll. "Ask me if you want accurate information."

Logan stared at the small creature. "Then . . . *you* tell me."

"There were nine males. Three were females, including their leader. I didn't hear her name, or anything they said. They were dressed in ancient costumes, all lace and velvety. Lovely, as I said." The doll gave him a tiny smile. "Now you know what we know."

And Bet ran off down the road with Judee.

Inside the shadowed house Logan walked into the master bedroom, to a tall oak dresser. He slid open the top drawer, removed a leather case, took a holster from the case.

Logan unsnapped the holster, slowly drew out the

Gun. Silver barrel. Pearl handle. Six chambers. He held it tightly in his hand.

He removed the ammopac from his tunic, snapping it into place. Immediately the Gun glowed, spilling a wash of pale gold across Logan's face and chest.

I swore I'd never use this again, he reminded himself, but now I'll use it. On them. On the ones who killed my son and took Jess. And I'll *enjoy* using it.

I'll find them.

And I'll use the Gun.

## BORGIAS

"We call them the Borgia Riders," said Jonath. He towered over Logan, a full foot taller, but without Logan's strength of body. The Wilderness leader was gaunt; his flesh hung loose on a bony frame, but his eyes were very alive, dark and penetrating.

They were walking together in warm morning sunlight outside the main camp, fronting the Lincoln Memorial. Jonath, in a gray workrobe, sashed at the waist; Logan, for the first time since Argos, wearing his Sandman's black tunic, boots and belt, the Gun holstered at his right side. He was a hunter once again, and he would wear the garb of a hunter.

"You know them?" Logan asked.

"I've never encountered them personally," said Jonath. "But some of the People have been attacked by them. They killed one of our men, and raped several of our women."

"Their leader's name . . . do you have it?"

"She calls herself Lucrezia."

"Know anything about her?"

"Only that she seems to possess a cruelty beyond

that of most outlanders. Human life apparently means very little to her."

Logan said nothing to this, but his eyes took on a hard shine.

"Still . . . Jessica may be alive."

"There's no reason to hope for that," said Logan flatly.

"But there is."

Logan suddenly stopped walking, stared at the Wilderness leader. "What are you saying? They'll use her sexually and they'll kill her."

"Perhaps," nodded Jonath. "But my point is—outlanders often trade the females they abduct. A beautiful woman can be quite valuable to them."

"And you think Jessica might—"

"—be traded off to a rich man, or to a Market group. Since the breakdown of the cities an extensive trade-sale Market has sprung up. Among the most salable items, next to certain drugs, are beautiful women."

"And outlanders have access to these markets?"

"They're prime suppliers."

Logan picked up a dry branch, snapped it in frustration. "But I don't know where to *look*. They could be halfway across country by now. I don't even know which direction they headed."

Jonath sat down on the squared base of a broken column which had once formed part of an ancient government building, ran his thumb slowly along the veined marble. "Logan, do you believe in the magic of the mind?"

Logan sat down next to Jonath, looked at him. "In what sense?"

"I believe that the human brain has infinite possibilities—that we've barely touched on our potential as fully developed creatures. Before the Little War, experiments were being conducted in telekinesis, telepathy, and a dozen other inter-related aspects of sensory phenomena. Brain expansion. . . . And one of these aspects was clairvoyance."

"I don't think I—"

"The ability to summon up visions involving a particular person, place or thing."

"I don't see what any of this has to do with me."

"There's an old man I've heard of . . . His name is Andar. He escaped the Sandmen. He lives at the tip of a bridge on the western coastline."

"So?"

"They call him 'The Gifted One.' He's physically blind, yet he *sees*. He's a visionary. He can 'read' objects."

*"Read* them?"

"Do you have something of Jessica's . . . a ring she wore . . . a throat jewel . . . anything of that nature?"

Logan nodded.

"Bring it to Andar. Ask him to read its vibrations. If what I've heard is true, he might be able to tell you where she is, physically, from his reading of the object."

"That's impossible!"

"I told you, he's a visionary. His mind is tapped into what he calls the 'cosmic energy source.' All objects in space are part of this cosmic chain. One object gives him a direct link to another."

Logan stood up. "This sounds insane."

"But you'll *do* it . . . You'll go to him?"

"Yes," said Logan. "I'll go."

# VISION

On the morning of April 16, 1988, twelve years before the Little War, the animals of San Francisco went mad. They howled, circled, twitched in fear . . .

Something was happening in the earth.

It began as a subterranean rumble, a stirring deep below the streets of San Francisco. God was clearing his throat. The rumble increased; earthplanes shifted; tall buildings swayed. Bay waters danced and rippled.

Then the people felt it—a movement beneath their feet, a rocking shimmer of motion which intensified by the second.

*Earthquake!*

The big one. The one all the seismologists had been predicting for decades. The San Andreas was loosing its century-stored pressures, and San Francisco was doomed.

Mass panic. Water mains erupted. Dams split. Boats were lifted and smashed against dock pilings. Automobiles were tossed like marbles from bridges and freeways.

And the *sounds* . . . The metal thunder of dying buildings, collapsing, tipping into the streets in slicing downfalls of stone and glass. The cry of tortured earth mixed with the agonized shriek of thousands as the land split wide to swallow them, their cars, their houses, their streets and their skyscrapers.

It lasted all of five minutes (although the aftershocks lingered for weeks). Atlantis-like, the city vanished beneath the iceblue waters of the Pacific, leaving only scattered island peaks as testimony that a great metropolis had once existed here.

The Golden Gate Bridge was one of these islands.

Most of the bridge was gone; under the assault of the quake, it had snapped its massive cables and whiplashed wildly, splitting its metal seams and plunging into the Bay. But the tip of the fabled structure remained above water, an immense tombstone of twisted metal, marking the death of a city.

Logan looked down at the ragged coastline. White-frothed waves beating at black rocks, cliffs of sun-washed stone rising up from the ocean's surge. And, just ahead, the ruins of the San Fran Complex . . .

As a Sandman, Logan had been taught that the only reality was the reality of the system, that the power of the Gun was paramount over the power of the mind. Mysticism was the work of demented misfits; it had no basis in fact. Yet, now, when he *should* have been using this precious time to search for Jessica, he was following a fool's dream, hoping that a blind old mystic could set him on the trail of the Borgias.

The trip from Washington had been frustrating. A mazecar would have whisked him here in minutes—but the overland flight took several days to complete. Still, the craft had performed beautifully on its long run, and for that Logan was grateful. Gyroparts were hard to come by, and any major repair would be difficult to effect.

He angled the paravane, bringing the ship closer to the water—until he was able to make out the rusted-orange South Tower of the bridge thrusting up, armlike, two miles out to sea.

Dia saw him coming. She moved close to her father, as close as she dared. "You told me a man would come, my father, and he is here. From the sky. He comes in black, like the night. He was once a Sandman. He wears their uniform."

"They pursued me," said the old man. "But I escaped them. I lived beyond their Guns. Now, it will be strange, helping one of them."

"This one is different. There are tales . . . He ran, fought the others, and killed many of them to save runners. He is called Logan."

"I help whoever comes to me," said the old man softly. "I make no exceptions. We are all one."

"I *see* him!" whispered Dia, exaltation in her voice. And she raised her blind eyes to the sky.

Descent required precision. The sharply-slanted fifty-foot segment of pitted steel offered no level terrain on which to land, and the shifting wind from the ocean struck the paravane like a heavy fist, tipping the craft at dangerous angles. If one of the blades clipped the bridge . . .

Logan set down, finally, cut power. The blades idled and died as he exited the control pod. He stood, chilled by the gusting ocean breeze, staring at the hut.

It was metaloid, squarish, much smaller than a city-unit. Crude, in fact. Andar and his people must have built it from bridge fragments. But why out here, in the middle of nowhere?

No one came to greet him. Not that Logan expected a formal welcome, but he *had* been told that Andar had two daughters, one of whom was with him. And that the old mystic stayed here always. Yet the hut—lashed to the remains of a ruptured support cable—was totally silent. It seemed deserted.

He moved closer, bracing his body against the wind tides. A wrong step on the slimed steel surface could take him over the side into the iced Pacific.

The hut's squat metal door stood open. Logan hesitated, then ducked his head and entered.

Darkness. After the glare of sky and water the dim interior seemed impenetrable—yet something glowed like fiery coals at the far end of the windowless structure.

A figure.

"Come forward, Logan," said the glowing figure.

Logan obeyed—until Andar's voice halted him.

"Not too close . . . Stop now! And do *not* attempt to touch me. There is no danger if proper distance is maintained. Have you been informed of my condition?"

"No," said Logan.

"I am blind, a victim of atomic fallout. My entire body surface has been affected. My skin is radioactive. I no longer feel heat nor cold. My flesh is insensitive to pain . . . Yet I must remain isolated to avoid contaminating others. Only my daughters can stay in my presence for long periods. They care for me."

"I understand," said Logan.

"Sit down, please. Dia, prepare a cushion."

A shadow-figure moved toward Logan; he squinted, trying to make out details, but his eyes had not yet fully adjusted to the dimness.

A bodycushion was placed near him. He sat down, sinking into it. "Thanks . . ." said Logan. "I—can't quite see you."

Musical laughter. "You have eyes, and I am without them—yet I see *you!*"

"My daughter, Dia," said Andar. "Both of my daughters have been blind from birth. They see, however, with the inner eye, and are thus graced."

"My sister, Liath, is on the shore," said Andar's daughter. "Yet she, too, sees you, Logan."

"Then you share your father's talents."

"Only to a degree," said the girl. "Even *our* sight is limited. We cannot deep-read vibrational auras as Father can. His gifts differ from ours."

Logan was now able to make out the girl, seated a few feet away from her father. A fall of long golden hair. A lean, curved body. Ivory skin. A delicate, piquant face. She wore a long robe of deep crimson, belted under the soft swell of her bosom.

"Now, tell me how I may help you," said the old man. He squatted on the bare cold flooring of the hut, totally nude, thin stick legs crossed beneath him, hands resting, palms-up, in his lap. His eyes, deep-caved, burned white in a narrow, hairless skull, and his glowing skin, stretched loosely over his bony frame like parchment illumined from within, was grooved and ravaged by time.

He was the oldest human Logan had ever seen.

"My young son was murdered by a group of outlanders called the Borgia Riders," said Logan. "They took my pairmate, Jessica." He hesitated. "I want to know if she lives, and *where* she is."

"And what have you brought me of Jessica?"

Logan took a small throatclasp from his tunic, started to hand it to Andar.

"No . . . place it at my feet."

Logan did this. He studied the mystic intently, wondering . . .

The old man picked up the clasp, spidered his long fingers over it, then enclosed the throat jewel in his right fist. He placed that fist against the center of his glowing skull, held it there, motionless.

*You have strong doubts that my father can help you . . . Please, Logan, don't doubt him. Allow yourself to trust. He will help you.*

Logan heard Dia's words, yet her lips had remained closed; no sound had issued from them.

A telepath. The only explanation. But, if she is, then is *he* also?

*No, Logan, my father reads vibrations but he does not read or send thoughts as Liath and I do. That is not his gift. You must speak aloud to him, as he to you.*

Logan was confused. *But I read your mind as you read mine, yet I am not telepathic.*

Her answer reached him instantly. *You are a parotelepath, which means you can mentally converse with one who is fully gifted, such as I am. I saw this talent in you the moment you entered my aura. Your mind is rich and strong. It could be raised to very high levels.*

These thought messages flickered between Logan and the girl in the space of a second, and human speech seemed suddenly cumbersome and unnecessary.

The old man said, "The vibrations have instructed me. I see your woman clearly."

Logan leaped to his feet. "Jessica's *alive?*"

"Sit down . . . listen to my words. Let me give you my sight."

Logan obeyed, heart pounding.

Andar spoke slowly. "She is with those you call the Borgia Riders. They . . . treat her unkindly, yet she lives."

"Where are they?" said Logan tightly. "Where do they have her?"

"That I cannot say," Andar told him. "My mind does not show me their location in exact terms."

"What terms then?" Logan's tone was demanding. "*Tell* me what you see!"

*Anger will not help you, Logan. Trust him . . . Allow him to guide you. Anger and impatience will only block the reception of my father's vision.*

Logan knew she was right. But it was almost impossible for him to be calm at this moment.

"I . . . receive many impressions . . . I *see* . . ." Andar's head fell forward on the thin stalk of his neck; he placed the tips of his fingers against his skull. His voice became high and lilting, as if in song, the words spaced and rhythmic:

**"Where . . . the rockets die . . . ..**
**and gantrys tilt . . .**
**against the sky . . .**
**where the plain is wide . . .**
**you will hear their cry . . .**
**as the Borgias ride."**

Logan drew in a long breath. "The Cape!" he said. "Cape Steinbeck in the Florida Keys. They must have a base there."

But Andar said nothing more. His head remained down, chin resting against his bony chest. His long hands were once again folded and motionless in his lap.

*My father sleeps. The use of his gift has tired him. You must go, Logan. He has told you all he can.*

"It's enough," said Logan. "I can *find* them now!"

## STEINBECK

A bleak plain of broken tarmac.

Rusting rocket gantrys.

Deserted bunkers.

Raw concrete blockhouses.

The Cape.

With the paravane out of sight beyond the open area, Logan moved steadily, at twilight, across the flat, weed-dotted plain of lifeless gray concrete.

He'd been here before when the Cape was alive and the Sanctuary rockets had flamed up for Darkside. Ballard had saved his life here—and, a decade later, had given his own to save others. A great man. A legend. Logan recalled the folkchant they used to sing about him . . .

*He's lived a double lifetime,*
*And Ballard is his name.*
*He's lived a double lifetime.*
*Why can't we do the same?*
*Ballard's lived a double lifetime,*
*And never felt no shame.*
*Think of Ballard.*

*Think of Ballard.*
*Think of Ballard's name . . .*

When the Sandmen had hit the Cape they'd destroyed all of Ballard's rockets in order to smash the Sanctuary Line. Logan passed them, the charred lifeships rusting in the Florida heat, their hulls ruptured by nitro blasts. These were the ships bound for Argos, ships which would have provided the vital supplies the space station needed to sustain life. In destroying them, the Sandmen had destroyed Argos as well.

But it was difficult for him to think of Argos, of the ships, even of Ballard . . . Logan's mind was focused on the job he had to do here—and one question hammered at him, obsessed him: *is she still alive?*

He *knew* the outlanders were here; he'd seen the glint of their jetcycs, rayed by dying sun, as he swung the paravane over the Cape. Now, he had a goal: the metal corpse of a giant freight rocket. She'd been designed for the Earth-to-Luna run, and they'd named her *Pequod,* after Ahab's fabled ship. Her ocean was space, her Whale the great white bulk of the Moon. She'd been the main link between Earth and the Darkside Colony before the station had been closed down and space travel aborted after the Little War.

And how does this proud star mammoth end her days? thought Logan. As headquarters for a depraved gang of psychopaths. Well, I'll flush the vermin from her metal cells. When I'm done today she'll be clean again.

Logan approached the *Pequod* at a defensive angle, staying close to the line of concrete bunkers, keeping inside the deeply cast twilight shadows. He could not afford being seen by any of the outlanders until he was actually inside the ship. From the air, Logan had counted more than ten cycles ranged outside the rocket, which meant he'd face up to a dozen riders. And beyond that, he didn't want to risk endangering Jessica if she was still their prisoner; they'd use her to stop him if they got the chance.

Logan had the Gun in his hand, feeling the power of the weapon. The hunter, again closing on prey . . .

Now, for the first time in many days, he allowed his mind to linger on the image of Jaq, stretched lifeless in the dark hallway of the Potomac house, victim of a rider's gun. He *wanted* to think of Jaq now, wanted to prime himself with fury, with vengeance fire . . . *Build the hate! Build the fury!*

They'd posted one of the riders as an outside guard. The fellow was big, rough-featured, dressed in a slash-velvet bodyshirt and laced Italian leggings; a heavy gold chain around his waist supported a holstered Fuser.

Logan ducked into a shadowed doorway, crouching there, wondering if he'd been seen.

He had the advantage, since the guard was obviously not expecting attack, lounging against one of the parked cycles, drinking from a chased-silver wine-flask, sleepy-eyed and half drunk.

Logan dropped him with a single blow, delivered from behind, just at the base of the rider's neck. The kill was soundless and brutally efficient.

Logan looked coldly down at the body, thinking: did you kill my son? He plucked the Fuser from the guard's chainbelt. A weapon like this did it. Maybe you *were* the one. Maybe.

Sound from within the rocket. Laughter. Wild, drunken voices. Good. They were having a party, meaning their reaction time would be sharply reduced by the intake of wine. He'd burn through them like god's lightning.

*But where was Jess?*

Locked away in another part of the ship? Sold or traded? Dead?

Logan would soon know.

Gun in hand, he moved into the rocket, toward the sound of Borgia laughter.

The *Pequod* was immense. Tier upon tier of storage compartments, a welter of cabins and intersecting walkways. Her hull was buttressed with great, curved-steel ribs, supporting a metal hide tough enough to deflect a direct hit by meteor. Built to last ten thousand years . . . and looking almost as new inside as the day they built her.

As Logan penetrated deeper into the great skyship he checked all of the compartments en route. No sign of Jessica.

But Andar had *seen* her here . . .

Closer now to the riders and their drunken revels.

Logan faded behind a bulkhead, flattened himself against the durosteel wall; someone was coming toward him. He waited.

It was one of the outlanders, probably sent to relieve the outside guard.

As he passed the bulkhead Logan snaked an arm around the man's neck, pulled him into an adjoining crew compartment. The rider's eyes bugged under Logan's killing pressure; he could not breathe.

"Talk to me or I'll kill you." Logan eased the pressure slightly.

"Wha'—what do you want?"

"The woman you took by the Potomac, in Old Washington . . . is she here?"

"No . . . not here."

"Where then?"

The rider twisted loose, going for the Fuser at his waist.

Logan broke his back.

He should have talked to me. But I would have killed him anyway.

He stepped over the rider's sprawled corpse. Logan

had two burnweapons, plus the Gun. The odds against him no longer mattered.

More laughter. He was almost on top of them. Another fifty feet, then an open hatchway. They were inside the main galley, at a long cooktable, eating, drinking wine—oblivious to the stalking hunter in black.

When Logan appeared in the hatchway all sound and movement ceased. He had holstered the Gun, and held a Fuser in each hand. "All weapons—on the table," he said.

There were nine riders facing him, two of them female. The men were armed with Fusers, the women daggers. They put these carefully on the cooktable, moving slowly, watching Logan. His face told them he was walking death.

"Which one of you leads?"

"I do," said Prince. There was a note of defiance in his voice. No one at the table challenged his statement.

Logan burned him down. Both barrels.

"Now," he said to the other eight riders. "I want to know about the female you took from the house on the Potomac. Who wants to tell me about her?"

The outlanders were stunned. They looked from Logan's eyes to the dead, blackened body of Prince.

"She *wanted* to come with us," said Ariosto. "Begged us to take her along, so we—"

A double blaze of burnfire. Ariosto crumpled forward across the table.

There was a smell of charred meat in the room.

"Someone else," said Logan in a deadlevel tone. "Talk. But only the truth."

The others were pale, slack-lipped, knowing that death was a heartbeat away for all of them.

"Prince wanted her . . . for himself," one of the females said, her voice unsteady. She kept wetting dry lips with her small, pink tongue.

"Prince?"

She nodded toward the first body.

"Go on."

"So we took her along. She was valuable. When . . . when Prince was . . . finished with her we . . . we knew we could get a good price for her on the Market."

"Who killed the boy?"

"Prince. With a Fuser."

"Where is the woman now?"

"After Prince took her here, Lucrezia decided to—"

"Lucrezia?" Logan looked at the other female, Ris. "That you?"

Ris shook her head, staring at him.

"Then who are you?"

Before an answer could be given one of the males lunged for a tabled Fuser, brought up the weapon in a short arc, triggered a laserburst.

Logan was hit in the right shoulder. The charge singed his flesh, and pain lanced his upper body. He dropped the weapon in his right hand as the arm went numb with shock. One of the females grabbed a dagger. Two other males had weapons now, and were firing at Logan.

They missed.

It was over very quickly. In a pain-blurred rage, Logan killed them all, staggered out into a passageway, collapsed against a metaloid strut. The second Fuser clattered to the ship's deck. He put back his head; a tight groan escaped his lips. The pain in his right shoulder was incredible. Fire lived in his flesh.

He knew he was vulnerable. He knew that the rider named Lucrezia was somewhere in the ship. But, at this second in time, he was incapable of active movement. The shock to his system was profound.

Logan slumped sideways to the deck. He raised his left fist, bit hard into the round of muscle below the thumb. To provide a new pain center, to counteract the blaze of agony from his shoulder.

He heard Lucrezia.

A scraping of feet, coming swiftly down a crew ladder from an upper ship-level. She'd be armed. And, if he stayed like this, she'd kill him.

*Get up!* His mind shouted at frozen muscles. *Unholster the Gun!* Can't. *You can!*

Only seconds now and she'd be here. He fumbled his left hand awkwardly over his belt, raised the holster flap, began dragging the Gun free.

He had it pointed at her when she rounded a final bend in the corridor. And he'd been right; she *was* armed—with a silver dagger of tempered Florentine steel.

"Drop it," said Logan tightly, looking up at her. He still could not stand.

"You're Logan, aren't you?" asked Lucrezia. She dropped the dagger—and smiled.

A beautiful woman. Deadly and beautiful. Her long court gown, cut low at the bodice, flowed with lace, stitched gold and silver.

"I'm Logan," he admitted.

"The others didn't think you'd follow us. I did. I thought you'd be here eventually."

"I'm here."

"Are they all—" She nodded toward the galley.

"All of them," he said.

She smiled again. "Just as well. They were a stupid lot. You can let me go. You have nothing to gain by killing me now."

"Why *should* I let you go?"

"In trade for information. About your Jessica."

Logan stirred, jaw tightening. "Tell me."

"Not unless you promise I can leave this ship alive."

"I make no promises to a Borgia!"

She shrugged, adjusted the hem of her gown. "Then kill me. And never learn the truth about your woman. I'm the *only* one who can tell you that truth."

"How do you know I won't kill you anyway?"

"You are a man of honor. I've heard about you, Logan. If you make a bargain, you keep it. Say you'll let me live and you'll have your truth."

"All right. You live."

She nodded. "Jessica is dead."

*Dead.*

The word almost blinded Logan with pain. His shoulder was nothing. Only the word was pain. And pain. And pain.

"How?"

"Prince killed her and burned the body. We came here with Jessica, intending to put her on the Market. But she was . . . stubborn. She caused trouble. Prince grew very angry with her. I couldn't do anything about it. I tried to save her—call it greed if you will—but unfortunately I did not succeed. I thought it a waste."

She turned away, began moving toward the outer hatch.

Logan watched her go.

*Die, you inhuman bitch!*

He triggered the Gun.

And the homer sang out.

## INTERIM

Logan did not remember flying the paravane back to Old Washington. The trip was blank and meaningless to him.

If he had found Jessica they could have shared the shock of their son's death together. Each would ease the other's loss, make it bearable. But Jess, too, was dead.

And Logan withdrew into himself as a sea creature withdraws into its shell. He talked to no one at the

Wilderness camp. He was mute and removed from the rhythms of their life.

Even Jonath could do nothing to bring Logan out of this self-imposed isolation.

The colony was struggling for bare survival. Food was hard-won from the earth; the carefully-nurtured crops gave meager reward for intense, protracted labor. Yet they *were* surviving, and that counted for something. With Jonath to guide them, the colony maintained a fragile wilderness stability.

Under his direction, the People had hollowed out a series of shallow caves below the Lincoln Memorial, and it was here, when cold and rain assaulted them, that they held out against the elements.

Logan's shoulder wound healed, but he never left the caves. He existed as an exile in the camp, sharing no labors, taking no part in the brief celebrations marking the birth of a new colony infant. He ate very little, and drank only when his tissues *demanded* water.

For Logan, the level of despair had reached maximum intensity; reality, without Jessica, was intolerable. He had to *totally* withdraw—but he needed help to do it.

One night, very late, with the camp asleep, he went to Jonath. The leader was sitting alone in his quarters under the Memorial, arranging seed pods for planting.

"I want them now," Logan said.

"No," the leader told him. "I can't, Logan."

"I can find Jess with them. It's the only way I'll ever have of finding her again. You *know* that."

"But in the dosage you propose the drugs are very dangerous. You'll be drawn completely into the past. Your body will be here, with us, but your mind . . ." He shook his head.

Logan said nothing.

"If you go back," said Jonath, "you may never emerge again, never regain present reality."

"I reject that reality," said Logan.

"And we don't know what the side effects will produce. No one has ever attempted to—"

"I want them," said Logan flatly.

"Even if I said yes, that you could have them, our supply here at the camp is limited. We use R-11 for medical aid, to ease mental pain, but in very small dosages. We couldn't spare anything like the amount you're asking for."

"Then I'll get it elsewhere," said Logan. "On the Market."

"That's your decision," nodded Jonath. "And I'd call it a very unwise one." His eyes held sadness. "I hate to see you do this, Logan."

"What difference does it make *what* I do?" Logan snapped. "I'm dead already without Jess. She's lost to me now, but she's still alive in my mind. With Jaq. All the years we had together are there. I want them back. I *must* find my wife and son again—and this is the only way."

"I still don't agree with what you're doing, but I understand it." Jonath sighed. "Do you know anything about the Market, how to contact it?"

"No, but it should be simple."

"Getting R-11 won't be. I know. I've tried to get it for the camp."

Logan was amazed. *"You* . . . on the Market?"

"The People are my responsibility," said Jonath. "I'll deal with *anyone* to help them."

"All right, so it won't be simple. How do I get R-11?"

Jonath hesitated. "I shouldn't be helping you do this to yourself."

"You'll help me."

"Only because there's no stopping you—whether I help or not."

"I'm glad you realize that," said Logan. His face was set.

"You'll have to go to the New York Complex. You'll never be able to get the amount you want locally."

"Who do I see there?"

"I don't know. But I can direct you to someone who does."

Jonath gave Logan the information.

By morning, the paravane was airborne.

## RAWLS

Summer heat in the Carolinas. Insect weather. Humid. Intense. A draining of the spirit. A punishment. Worse now, since the cities died. No way to escape the scalding air. No coolvents, no frostflow piped into snug lifeunits. Just the heat, lying heavy on Carolina earth, sapping energy and the will to move.

Rawls 7 hated it, cursed it. But without legs, you don't do much traveling. People came to him; he didn't go to them. And Darlington, South Carolina, was where they came.

Rawls hated more than the weather. Most of all, he hated being a cripple. When the Complex died he'd been trapped in a slideway; two of the knife-edged friction belts had snapped, lashing at him like thick steeloid snakes. The main belt caught him just below the waist, slicing off both legs with the precision of a Mark J Surgeon. Miracle he didn't bleed to death. Another citizen had used medseal on him, and that stopped the bleeding in time. But the legs were gone.

Females wouldn't touch him now. Called him a freak. What irony! Rawls, the glasshouse king, whose sexual exploits had been the talk of Arcade—reduced to a loveless cripple.

But, as a prime touchman on the Market, Rawls still had power. He was shrewd. He knew how to finger things people wanted, knew the wheres and the hows and the whos. If you wanted a hard-to-find item in the Market you came to Rawls. To the small shack squatting in humid heathaze on the Daytona Turnpike.

As Logan did.

"Jonath sent me," he said to the legless man. "I need R-11, a lot of it, and he said you'd know where to get it."

Logan stood just inside the doorway. The place smelled foul—and the stubble-bearded little man on the dented groundcart exhaled the same fetid odor.

"How much do you need, citizen?"

"A quantampac. Full dex."

Rawls rubbed the stump of his right leg with grimed fingers. "You know, I can still feel the *whole* damn thing. Clear to the toes. Knee, muscles, tendons . . . Left one, I can't feel. Just the right one. But they're *both* gone. How do you figure a thing like that?"

"I don't," said Logan. He waited, looking steadily down at Rawls. "Well?"

"Can't get a quantam short of NY," he said.

"I'll go there," Logan said.

"Why do you need so much?"

"That's my business."

"Going to use it yourself?"

"Maybe."

"Long lift in a quantam," mused Rawls, scrubbing at the stubble on his cheek. "Long, long lift."

"I know what I need," said Logan. "You just tell me where to get it."

Rawls palmed a powerstud on his skimmer, and the rusted groundcart flowed him to a corner of the room. He attempted to open the lower drawer of a cabinet. The door wouldn't budge. Rawls banged at it with the heel of his right fist. "Heat swells the wood, makes it stick," he told Logan. "Heat ruins everything."

Logan watched him, his face expressionless.

Rawls finally got the drawer open, scrabbled inside for a black, lifeleather foilbook. Then he wheeled back to Logan.

"In here," he said, tapping the book, "I've got the name of a contact who can sell you as much R-11 as you need. But first . . ."

"You want to be paid."

"Exactly."

"I was told you could use these." And Logan opened a tab-box, shook several magnetic skinjewels onto a wooden table. "With each mood, an individual's body chemistry is altered, and these change color to reflect that mood. They belonged to—" (*Jessica. I can see her wearing them.*) "—a female I knew. Skinjewels were quite popular in the Angeles Complex."

"Heard about them," said Rawls. "Never saw any." He plucked a shining red heartstone from the table. It deepened to a festered green in his hand. "How many have you got?"

"These. No more."

"And what will you use for trade in New York?"

"That's not your concern," said Logan. "Do we have a deal or don't we?"

Rawls swept up the stones, quickly pocketed them. "Your contact," he said, handing Logan a foilslip from the book. "Show this when you get there."

Logan took it, started out.

The legless man followed him, wheeling from the shack into bright sunlight. "I can always use *more* of these," he said as Logan walked toward the paravene.

Rawls shaded his eyes against the heat-scald, receiving no answer. He watched the black-garbed figure climb into the control pod, activate the blades. Debris whipped and danced around the cripple in the agitated air as the paravane built power.

The craft lifted, was gone.

Rawls shifted the stones inside his pocket with slow fingers.

In the heat, his missing right leg began to ache.

## GIANT

Logan had taken a mazecar to the New York Complex on leave from DS school when he was sixteen to pairmate with a female who lived there. She was an older woman of twenty, a year away from Sleep and into young Sandmen. Gonzales 2 had told Logan about her, told him she was something really special. Chinese. Sexually astonishing.

Gonzales had been correct. Her voracious sensual appetites had drained Logan, left him anxious to return to duty. The pleasure with her had been so intense it was akin to pain. New York was different then: glittering, swarming with citizens, a world mecca for exotic living.

Now it was a dark ruins.

But it had something Logan wanted far more than he had wanted the Chinese girl. It had R-11.

In 1997, when Mayor Margaret Hatch had ordered the Central Park fill-in, construction of the Green Giants had begun. Taking their name from the fact that they were replacing the last bit of open greenery in New York City, the Giants were designed to accommodate three million, a bold step in reducing the city's acute housing crisis. In height, they were taller than the Empire State and each was a self-contained miniature city, with every comfort and convenience. To get space in one, you hocked your soul, and signed a lifetime lease.

The first three-mile complex was a converted Giant. But, eventually, the outdated skytowers were torn down and replaced.

Nostalgia prevailed. As a memorial to the past, one of the Green Giants was allowed to remain standing, dwarfed by the three-mile city dwellings around it.

Yet it lived again when the Thinker died. Its pre-computerized, self-contained power units were quickly utilized, and it became the hub in cross-state Market operations, a mighty storehouse-headquarters, humming with activity. After more than a century of obsolescence, it was now the only living structure in a dead city.

Logan came to the Giant for R-11.

Jonath had told him that he would have no trouble with Scavengers in New York. This was one city they did not control. "The Marketers are in charge there," Jonath had said.

"Who are they exactly?"

"Mostly ex-DS. A few key merchantmen. They keep the Scavengers in line. The city's wide open."

Flying over it at night, Logan got the impression of a vast, lightless range of man-made mountains, upthrusting peaks of steel and glass. Dominating the interior of the city, with flamebright gaudiness, standing two thousand feet above street level, light flooding out from its metal pores, stood the Green Giant.

As he swept over the shining structure, pinlights found his craft. Two Market patrolships soared up from the roof of the building to circle Logan, guiding him to a setdown on the Giant's illumined skyport.

Logan cut power, exited to the roof.

"No weapons allowed," a tall man in gray said to him. The Market guard carried a belted Fuser. His eyes were humorless.

Logan nodded, placed his holstered Gun inside the

paravane, sealed the magnetic lock. "How long can I leave my ship here?" he asked.

"As long as you have business inside," said the guard. "We'll keep an eye on it."

"Thanks," said Logan.

Another gray-clad guard walked up to him as he neared the entrance shaft. "Name?"

"Logan 3."

"Seeing who?"

"Lacy 14."

"You'll need a contact pass."

Logan handed him the foilslip he'd obtained from Rawls. The guard studied it for a moment, notched one corner with a foilpunch, handed it back.

"Go ahead," he said, activating the shaft release.

Logan stepped inside.

The interior corridors shimmered with light; this intensity of artificial illumination stunned Logan. He'd seen nothing like it since the days of Arcade. Because the Giant was able to generate its own electricity, and had never depended on the Thinker for power, the death of the great computer had not affected it. Restoration had been relatively simple—and now this city-within-a-city was functioning at peak efficiency after long years of darkness. Indeed, a sleeping Giant had awakened to serve new masters.

Although the outer surface of the building glowed beacon-bright, the majority of its two hundred floors were dark; the Market occupied only the Penthouse area, and the three floors just beneath for storage. The Giant was private, off-limits, except to those who ran the Market, and to the few special customers allowed to deal inside for highgrade goods. Such as R-11.

At the end of the corridor another guard stopped Logan. Same gray uniform. Same eyes. The hard look of the Sandman. Ex-DS, fitting their new roles as skin fits muscle.

"Pass," said the guard.

Logan produced the notched foilslip.

The guard pressed a section of wall. A door oiled back.

"Keep moving," said the guard.

Another corridor. Much shorter.

Logan faced a heavy flexcurtain, woven entirely from gold mesh. The curtain stirred, folded back.

"Come in, Logan 3."

A woman's voice. Sensual. Low-pitched.

Logan entered a chamber draped in silks and lit by firebirds. The small, feathered creatures, whose metallic bodies pulsed with inner light, swooped in glowing arcs around the large center room, settling, strutting, ruffling their multicolored plumage . . .

Logan hesitated, scanning the room. He saw no one. Only the birds, like moving fire jewels.

Then the woman appeared, rising from one corner of the chamber. She had been lying on a fall of snowpillows and, in standing, seemed to materialize from the room itself, seemed made of silks and smoked ivory.

Her body was perfection—a rich orchestration of scented peaks and soft valleys, tautly accented by the white flowgown she wore. A cat-emerald burned at her throat.

"I'm Lacy 14," she said.

"Since you know my name," said Logan, "I assume you also know what I came for."

A firebird fluttered to her shoulder and she stroked the glowing plumage, her large green-black eyes fixed on Logan.

"Why so abrupt?" she smiled. "I never conduct business without getting to know my buyers. Sit down, Logan."

Snowpillows. A soft peltrug of worked silver. No couch or chairs. Logan sat, adjusting one of the larger pillows at his back.

"Much better," said Lacy. "Drink?"

"No."

"I insist. I have a really excellent fruitwine from Spain which is impossible to duplicate," she told him.

Logan nodded. "Since you insist."

She brought him the wine, settled next to him. "Let us drink to the satisfactory conclusion of pleasure."

Logan was edgy, off-balance; he had expected a hard-faced Marketer who would waste no time, no words. He'd expected to deal quickly and be gone without ceremony. But, instead, here was Lacy . . .

Logan tasted the wine, allowing the smoked flavor to permeate his tongue. "You're right," he said. "This is excellent."

"I've heard about you, Logan."

"What have you heard?"

"That you sought out and destroyed the Borgias. Alone, at Steinbeck. One against twelve. Is it true?"

"It's true," said Logan. "But I'm not going to talk about it."

"That's not necessary," she smiled. "You're obviously a man of great passion. I've . . . been waiting for someone extraordinary."

Logan slipped a sack of Mooncoins from his belt.

"All I want here is what I came to get," he said. "A quantampac of R-11."

"That will be produced in due course. After you've earned it."

"I have these," he said, handing her the Mooncoins. "There's nothing like them on Earth."

She put the sack aside, unopened. "We'll deal with these later. *I* come first."

Logan was suddenly angry.

"Get a merchantman to penetrate you," he said. "Or one of your ex-DS. They all have fine bodies. They'll do a very satisfactory job."

She laughed, a throaty sound, deep and assured. "I

don't want you—or any other male," she told him. "I never allow a man to touch me. Ever."

"Well, what *do* you want?"

"Follow me and find out." She stood, putting aside her wine.

Logan got up. "Can't we just—"

"This way," said Lacy. "If you want the pac, you do as I say."

Sighing, Logan followed her out of the chamber.

They moved together down a short hallway. Lacy opened a mirrored door, beckoned Logan forward.

The room he entered was a large bedchamber, draped in crimson and gold. Soft lights shone through the draperies, and at least half of the floor area was occupied by two deep, expansive flowbeds.

"Recline," said Lacy. "On the farther bed. I'll take this one."

Logan did as she asked. What did she have planned for him? . . .

Lacy kept her eyes on Logan as she touched a magclasp at her neck; the gown fell away from her body in a soft spill of white. "Am I not beautiful?" she asked him.

"You are," he said.

Her breasts were coned and delicate, tapering to a waist which swelled to perfect hips and long, superbly-muscled legs. "Many men have desired me. Do you desire me, Logan?"

"At another time, in another place . . ."

She draped herself across the bed, facing his, cat-smiled at him. "I am not your concern here," she said. "You shall provide a show . . . for my stimulation."

"I don't understand."

She clapped her hands sharply.

The drapes parted at the rear of the chamber.

There were three of them. All nude. All beautiful. All black-skinned and full-figured and arousing. Perfect females, who would have been the pride of any glasshouse from Moscow to Paris.

"They're for you, Logan," said Lacy. "And you are for them."

"You expect me to—"

"Pleasure them. That's what you shall do if you want to please me. And if you do *not* please me, you will not get the thing you came for."

She turned to the girls. Her eyes were bright and hot. "Undress him," she said. "Caress him. Erect him."

They swayed toward Logan like dusky flowers.

So *this* is how she obtains her satisfaction? All right, Logan told himself, I'll do as she asks. I'll give her a show. And I'll enjoy what I'm doing. I'll steep myself in warm flesh . . . lose myself in sexuality.

Indeed, why not?

And Logan took them into his arms.

## PEARL

Logan followed Lacy 14 down the short hallway. As they entered her living quarters a firebird settled on Logan's shoulder, splashing his face with vivid colors. He shook the bird off, and the creature wing-whispered away.

"I did what you asked," he said to Lacy.

"A splendid performance," she agreed. She was wearing the white gown once again, and it billowed as she turned.

"Do I get the pac now?"

"Let me see what you've brought." She picked up the sack of Mooncoins, spilled them into her hand. They were round, bright, stamped with Moon symbols.

"I brought them down from Darkside," said Logan. "You won't find any others. Anywhere."

"They're . . . attractive," she said. "I can use them. But they won't pay for a full dex. Not of R-11."

Logan flushed with anger. "I did what you asked with the females . . ."

"And enjoyed yourself handsomely in the process," she said.

"Wasn't that what you wanted—to watch me pleasuring them to pleasure yourself?" He tightened his jaw. "I've given you all I have. Everything."

"Not everything," she said.

"What's left?"

"Your paravane. It should fetch a good price. I'll take the coins, *and* your ship." She smiled. "You know, I'm really being generous about this. You're here alone, unarmed. Normally, I would just have my men *take* your ship and give you nothing in return. But . . . since you've . . . amused me, I'm willing to turn over the drug."

"I can't get back to camp without my ship," said Logan. "And I *need* Jonath. It's impossible to take R-11 without someone to—"

"Take it here," said Lacy. "I'll provide a liftroom for you, and see to your needs."

Logan considered it. There was nothing left for him in Old Washington. Why *not* stay here in the New York Complex? One city was no better or worse than another now, without Jess.

"I accept," said Logan.

"There's risk in a full dex," said Lacy. "It could kill you."

Logan said nothing.

"There's no body or mind control with such a high dosage," she said. "You're at the mercy of the drug."

"I want maximum lift," said Logan. "A *full* re-live. And only a dex will give me that."

"Your decision," shrugged Lacy. "Get whatever personal belongings you have in the ship, then come back here. I'll have the R-11."

He hated losing the paravane. It was a high price to pay. Still, Lacy could have simply taken it, as she said. In dealing with the Market there were no guarantees. You took what they gave you.

Logan had the Gun when the guard said, "You can't go back inside with that." His name was Stile, and he captained Lacy's men. Huge. Slab-bodied. Cruel-faced.

"Lacy made the deal," said Logan. "She gets the ship and I get my personal belongings. This is mine. It goes with me."

Stile looked sullen. "All right . . . I'll make an exception this time," he said. "But keep it holstered."

"Couple of Fusers in there you can have," said Logan. "They were never mine to begin with."

He fixed the Gun holster to his belt.

There was nothing else. The ship was theirs now.

As the R-ll would soon be his.

The small liftroom was stark and empty, dun-colored, without ornament or decoration. Four walls, a floor and a ceiling. No windows or vents.

"You'll need this," Lacy said, and gestured. A gray-clad guard dumped a bodymat, quickly unrolled it. The mat covered the floor, wall to wall.

"What about oxygen?"

"Enough. The room's not sealed."

"I'll need water."

"At necessary intervals. Pelletgun . . . directly into your system."

"I don't want to be observed," said Logan.

"You won't be," said Lacy. "But if you convulse . . ."

"*No* observation. Just the injections . . . water when I require it. Agreed?"

"Agreed."

"The drug?" asked Logan.

From her belt, Lacy withdrew a small silver disc. She pressed its center and the disc released a single milky-white pearl. It rolled, catching the light, in the palm of her hand.

"Hard to believe that's a full dex," said Logan.

She smiled. "You've never used R-11?"

"No," he admitted.

"A normal dosage is almost microscopic," she told him. "This is a quantam, full-dex strength. Usually this much R-11 is broken into powder, administered in several stages. I've never seen anyone take a pearl."

"The Re-Live drawers died with the cities," said Logan. "This is the only way left to go back."

"Is going back *that* important?"

"Yes," said Logan. "It's that important."

She looked at him for a long moment, then handed him the pearl.

"Just place it in the middle of your tongue," she said. "Let it dissolve directly into the tissue. It's effective immediately after ingestion."

And she left him.

# LIFT

Logan brought up the pearl, holding it between the thumb and index finger of his right hand; he studied it in the subdued light of the room. Harmless looking. Beautiful in its simple perfection.

But potent. Very, very potent.

The surface-distortion drug he'd been given by the Scavengers was Candee next to R-11, which was designed to penetrate to the deepest levels of stored life-experience. Science had long since proven, beyond any doubt, that every experience, however trivial, is permanently retained: every sight, sound, odor, every sensory moment of touch, every spoken word . . . all there, all three-dimensionally alive in the depths of the human brain.

The Re-Live parlors were built on this principle. In their metal wombs it had been possible to re-experience, at choice, any hour, or day, or moment of one's past.

That was the key word: *choice*. The Re-Live drawers gave you selective control, provided you wished to exercise it. And there were built-in shutoffs if the emotional surge threatened body-health. A Re-Live drawer was safe.

Not so with R-11. At maximum dosage, there was no control; it prowled the vaults of memory at will, and all choice was removed. However, short of maximum, Logan was not certain he could reach his full experiences with Jaq and Jessica. Under a light dosage he might never find them again.

R-11 had one basic advantage over any other mind-drug. It gave back *truth,* not fantasy; experiences, not hallucinations. It did not distort as Lysergic Foam did. What Logan re-lived would be *real* events from his past.

And, buried in that past, his wife and son waited for him.

Logan sat down on the mat which gave softly under his weight.

Now.

Pearl into mouth. On the tongue. Dissolving . . .

Logan was fighting for balance. The wind whipped at his tunic, fisting him with short, savage gusts. He wasn't sure he could maintain his footing—and a fall was death.

He was sixteen, and new to DS. A raw Sandman, just out of Deep Sleep Training, hunting his first female, nervous, and over-anxious to prove himself.

Logan's runner, Brandith 2, had glass-danced the Arcades before her flower blacked; she was extremely agile, with an incredible sense of body-control. She had lured her nervous pursuer onto a narrow outside repair-ramp, dipping and weaving her way along the thin ridge of metal ahead of him. Luring him forward.

*You should have fired the homer; the homer would have finished her!*

In his excitement, Logan had set the Gun at ripper, and to be effective a ripper must be fired at fairly close range. He could re-set for homer, but to do so would require taking both hands off the ledgerail, and that was impossible. He'd lose his balance for sure.

"What's the matter, Sandman?" her voice mocked him. "Can't you catch me?"

She had passed an angle-beam, and was no longer in direct sight. Logan moved faster along the ramp, reached the beam. She was waiting for him.

"You're dead, Sandman!" And, braced on the beam, Brandith 2 delivered a smashing blow to his chest with her left foot.

Logan swayed, pitched forward to his knees. The Gun slipped from his clawing fingers. He twisted, hooking his right arm into a strut-support, and slashed up with the heel of his left hand.

The surprise blow took Brandith 2 at throat level, and crushed her windpipe. She clutched at her neck, gasped blood, and fell over the edge in a long, screaming death drop.

Logan felt relief, and instant shame. He'd failed to homer her, and worse yet—much worse—he'd lost the Gun. A Sandman must *never* relinquish his weapon: the first rule of DS. And now he had allowed a female runner to disarm him, and almost kill him.

On the ramp, alone in the crying wind, Logan could

not move. He was locked into his misery. "Failure!" he said aloud. "Failure!"

Would he *ever* deserve to wear the uniform of a Sandman?

Egypt was a bore.

Logan was eight, and had taken a robocamel to the Pyramids with his best friend, Evans 9. They'd been to Japan earlier that morning, and found Kyoto dull with its restored temples and fat, bronze deities. But, in Tokyo, a sumo wrestler had taught them how to immobilize an opponent by a theatrical display of aggression, without actual body contact. Fascinating.

But Egypt was all heat and endless sand and ugly-snouted robot camels. The Pyramids were a disappointment—smaller than Logan expected, and badly in need of repair. The surface was pitted and crumbling, with many large stones near the top missing entirely.

"They ought to fix them," said Logan. "Smooth them out."

"No, tear them down," said Evans. "Put up new ones, *better* ones. Old things aren't worth saving."

"Old things are ugly," said Logan.

And that night they took a mazecar to Uganda.

"I can leave here, go with you," she told him.

"No, that's not possible."

"Why isn't it?"

"Because it isn't."

"But you find me exciting? You enjoy my body?"

"Yes."

"Then we'll pair-bond. Until it goes bad. When it goes bad, I'll leave. What's wrong with that?"

"A lot," he said. "I live alone."

"Why?"

"Because of what I am."

This silenced her.

The lovelights of the glasshouse played over their bodies. Gold . . .

Silver . . .

Red . . .

Yellow . . .

Blue . . .

And still she did not speak.

When Logan left the glasshouse he was angry. Why *couldn't* he form an alliance? Why *must* he live alone, finding sexual satisfaction on this fragmented, impulse basis?

*Because of what I am.*

A DS man cannot function effectively if he is pair-bonded. All emotional ties must be severed. Commitments must not be made. Nothing must interfere with duty.

Duty.

Duty.

"Show me your hand, Logan," said the psyc doctor.

Logan obeyed.

"Do you know why you have this?" he said, tapping the palmflower with an index finger.

"To tell my age," Logan said.

"And how old are you?"

"I'm six."

"And what happens when you're seven?"

Logan looked down at his palm. "It goes to blue. And I . . . leave Nursery."

The doctor nodded. He had kind eyes. "And you are afraid?"

"Yes," said Logan.

"Why? Why are you afraid, Logan?"

The words spilled out in a rush: "Because I love my talk puppet and because I don't want to leave Nursery and because . . ."

"Go on, tell me."

"Because the world is so big and I'm so little."

"But every boy and girl feels that way, and *they're* not afraid."

"I'll bet *some* of them are," said Logan. "Or they wouldn't use a machine like you."

"I deal with many problems at Nursery," said the doctor. He whirred to a medcab, took out a packet of Candees.

"I don't want a Candee," said Logan.

"But they taste good and they make you feel good," said the doctor.

"They make me sleepy."

"Take a Candee, Logan."

"No."

*"Do as I say!* Take one."

"No."

Logan backed away, but the square machine whirred after him. The doctor's kind eyes were no longer kind. They glittered with determination.

"I'll report this to Autogoverness," he threatened. "You'll be punished."

"I don't care," said Logan defiantly.

"Very well," said the doctor. And he pushed a button on his desk.

An Autogoverness rolled into the office.

"Logan 3 is to be punished. After punishment, he will be given a Candee."

"Yes, doctor," said the round, many-armed robot. She took Logan's hand in one of hers.

"You see, Logan," said the doctor as the boy was being led out. "You *can't* win."

"How long has he been under?" asked Lacy.

"Two days, six hours," said Stile.

"Convulsions?"

"Minor so far."

"Heartbeat?"

"Erratic, but holding."

"Skincount?"

"One over fifteen. The chemical balance is distorted, but not critical. Of course, he's going in deeper. It could get worse. No way of telling."

"If he dies, notify me immediately."

"Of course," said Stile.

The blow caught Logan at the upper part of the shoulder, a deltoid chop, delivered with force and precision. He felt his left arm go numb, angled his body sharply to keep Francis in direct line of attack.

He lashed out with a reverse savate kick, catching Francis at rib-level, causing him to lurch back, gasping for breath.

"You're good, Logan," said the tall, mantis-thin man, slowly circling his opponent.

"You're better, damn you!" Logan said. "But I'm learning."

"More each day," agreed Francis. "Shall we end this?"

Logan nodded, rubbing his shoulder. "I've had enough."

They hit the needleshower, standing together silently in the cutting spray. Francis had paid for his reputation; his body, in contrast to Logan's unmarked one, bore the scars of a hundred near-death encounters with fanatic runners, cubs, gypsies . . . Of the crack DS men at Angeles Complex, Francis was the fastest, the most dangerous, the best. Logan was still his pupil, but soon he might be his equal—with natural talent, good fortune, supreme dedication.

Francis had all these.

They walked back into the combat room, got into fresh grays.

"There's a lift-party tonight at Stanhope's," said Logan. "Why not unbend, take it in?"

Francis smiled thinly. The smile was bloodless. "I don't party," he said.

"But we're off-duty until—"

"A Sandman's never off-duty," said Francis coldly. "We could be called in for backup."

"That's never happened to me yet," declared Logan.

"It might," said Francis.

Logan looked at him. "What *do* you do with your free time?"

"Use it properly. I don't waste it on witless females and lift parties."

"I give up," sighed Logan. He grinned. "You know, Francis, I wouldn't be surprised to find little wires and cogs and springs under your skin . . . You're not *quite* human."

"I get my job done," said Francis stiffly.

"Sure. Sure you do," said Logan. "Forget what I said."

But, as he watched Francis walk out, Logan wondered: what the hell *does* he do with his free time?

"This one's dangerous," said Evans. "He's stolen a paravane and he's got a Fuser with him. I think we need backup."

Logan agreed. "Get on it, while I see if I can run him down."

"With a stick? Can you handle one?"

"I've ridden them before," said Logan. "They're much faster than a paravane."

"Take care," said Evans, sprinting for a callbox.

Logan checked his ammopac. Full load. He could use a nitro on the runner's ship if he had to. He kicked the hoverstick into life, soaring up at a dizzy angle. Too much thrust. He throttled down a bit, gained full control, gradually increasing his airspeed.

The runner's paravane had been tracked at dead center on the Kansas/Missouri line—which meant if he cut through Greater KC Logan should intercept near the Jefferson Complex.

The Missouri River rolled below him, brown and

sluggish. A few speedtugs, a private sailjet or two, otherwise the river was undisturbed. It didn't worry about runners or callboxes or backups or devilsticks or Sleep. Old Man River . . . just keeps rolling along.

Logan had been correct in his calculations. He spotted the stolen paravane just past Jefferson. Moving at full bladepower.

The runner saw Logan bearing in, swung his ship to face the new threat.

He's bringing up the Fuser! Time to show him what you can do with a stick.

The runner fired.

And missed.

And fired again.

Logan was a sun-dazzled dragonfly—darting, dipping, swooping erratically. An impossible target.

He unholstered the Gun.

The paravane rushed at him.

Logan had the charge set at nitro. *Now!*

The runner and his ship erupted into gouting, blue-white flame. The stricken craft tipped over and down, diving into Missouri earth with a roar.

Logan brought the stick in, dismounted, checked the runner. Nothing left of him but his right arm and hand, jutting grotesquely out of the flame-charred control pod.

Centered in his palm: a black flower.

"Any change?" asked Lacy.

"He's worse," said Stile. "Into severe muscle convulsions. Skincount's up. And his heart is taking a beating."

"He can't go on, then?"

"He's a hard man," Stile said. "He might surprise you."

They were waiting at Darkside, where their rocket was being readied for the jump to Argos—and Logan held Jessica close, telling her how much he loved her, telling her he'd never known that it was possible to experience such intense emotion, such care-bonding.

"We're free now," she told him. "We can live without fear, build a life together, raise children, be thirty, forty, fifty . . ."

He smiled, touched at her hair. God, but she was lovely!

"I want a son," he told her.

"We'll have him," she said, squeezing Logan's hand.

"And he'll have children of *his* own . . . and we'll be . . . what did they call them?"

"Grandparents," she said. "Grandma and Grandpa."

Logan chuckled, shaking his head. "That's hard to believe, to accept. No dreams. No fantasies. A *real* life ahead of us on Argos."

"Ballard said it wouldn't be easy there," she reminded him. Her eyes clouded. "I wish—"

"What?"

"—that Ballard could have come with us. We *need* a man like that on Argos."

"He's needed more on Earth," said Logan. "To handle the Sanctuary Line. To help more runners."

"I know," she nodded. "We owe him our lives."

"Everybody here owes him the same debt," said Logan.

And, touching, they stared out beyond the port, at the chalked, lifeless horizon of the Moon.

When Jaq was five Logan and Jess gave him a special party. Only the spaceborn were invited—those who had been conceived on Argos and who, like Jaq, had never known their mother planet.

Logan told the children about Earthgames he'd played in Nursery, about vibroballs and teeter-swings and talk puppets. It seemed they could never hear enough about Earth.

"Were there really Sandmen who chased you?" asked a girl of six.

Logan nodded.

"And were the Sandmen really bad?" asked the little girl.

"Yes," said Logan. "But they were taught to be. Some of them changed . . . They didn't all stay bad."

"You were one, weren't you?" asked a ten-year-old, eyes alight.

"I was one," admitted Logan.

"And were you bad?"

"For awhile."

"No!" screamed little Jaq, running across the chamber to his father, hugging him fiercely. "Logan was *never* bad!"

The boy was sobbing.

Jessica came to them, held them both. She kissed Logan's cheek.

In the sudden, strained silence a six-year-old tugged at Logan's wrist.

"Can we play now? *Can* we?"

"He's calmer," said Stile. "Relaxed. Almost tranquil. His mind seems to have found what it was looking for. He's in very deep."

Lacy looked pensive. "What do you think a Sandman's Gun would bring on the Market?"

"A great deal. But it would have to be de-fused, the pore-pattern detonation device neutralized."

"Can that be done?"

"It can be. It's a very delicate procedure."

She paced the room, thinking.

"He'll never trade or sell the Gun," said Stile.

"I know," she said. "It won't be possible to negotiate with him." She stopped, looked directly at Stile. "We'll have to kill him."

## OUT

Sprawled face-down across the mat, deep in his mental dreamworld with Jessica and Jaq, Logan was not aware that the room had changed, that something was being *added* to the atmosphere. From a small opening under the door a colorless substance was being piped into the chamber.

Tetrahyde. Toxic and totally effective on human bodytissue. Once absorbed into the lungs, it destroyed them with deadly efficiency.

Logan breathed in . . . breathed out . . . breathed in . . .

He had exactly ten more minutes of life.

*Logan, Logan, do you hear me?*

*I . . . hear you.*

*You are in great danger. You must come out!*

*No. Here with Jessica . . . with Jaq.*

*Listen to me, Logan. It's Dia.*

*How? How did you find me?*

*Jonath. When you didn't return to the camp he sent word to me. He knew no one else could reach you.*

*Where—are you now?*

*Close to you. Close to the Giant. I knew they'd never let me see you—so I'm sending my mind to you, my thoughts . . . You must come out to me!*

*No. Won't come out.*

*They're killing you, Logan.*

*Not true. They help me, give me water . . .*

*All that's over. The woman, Lacy, she has made up her mind to take the Gun. I know her thoughts . . . she wills you dead. Poison is in the air. You must come out, now! I'll help you . . . our two minds, together . . . Only minutes remain!*

Logan willed his body to fight the drug—and Dia linked her mind to his; the images inside Logan's head began to mix, break up . . .

. . . and Jessica was . . .
the Loveroom, and "Mother loves you," said Ballard . . .
who was Francis, who was . . . Jaq, only five, but already he . . .
kissed her deeply, knowing they were never going to . . .

*Harder! Try harder, Logan!*
*Trying. Can't. No use.*
*Fight! Break free!*

. . . because Box was . . . in the cave . . .
falling . . .
and love was . . .
fa
l
l ing . . .
everything w
a
s fa
l
l
i
n
g
.
.
.

*No. Too deep . . . too far in . . .*
*But you're doing it . . . we're doing it together . . . you're almost . . .*
*. . . out!*

Logan blinked stupidly; his head pounded—as if a thousand hot needles had been driven into his skull.

*Only a few seconds left! Use the Gun, Logan! Use it!*

Logan fumbled dizzily at his belt holster, his nostrils filled with the acid odor of Tetrahyde . . . The gas was upon him. He held his breath, pulled the Gun free . . .

Fired.

The nitro charge exploded the door from its hinge-locks, flooding the liftroom with fresh air.

Logan staggered to his feet, plowed across the mat toward the gaping exit.

*Where are you, Dia?*

*Outside. On the street just below the Giant. You'll see me.*

*I'll be there. Soon.*

Stile was in the corridor, running toward Logan, a weapon in his hand.

Gun on ripper.

Logan fired, tearing him apart.

Lacy saw this, darted back into her chambers. The firebirds cawed and fluttered.

Gaining strength by the second, Logan swept past her, reached the outside door, raced for the roofport.

Behind him, Lacy was screaming: "Stop him! Stop him!"

Three guards tried to—without success. Logan chopped them aside with blows from Gun and body.

Lacy appeared in the roof door, Fuser in hand, firing as Logan reached his paravane. Her first beam-blast sheared away a section of alum sheeting next to Logan's head.

He swung bitterly toward her, triggered the Gun, on tangler.

The swift whirl of steelmesh filament engulfed her—and she fell back, clawing at the choking, constricting coils of metal.

Dia was not alone when Logan reached her. The man from the Wilderness camp who had flown her to New York was there.

"How did you find another paravane?" Logan asked him.

"There are still a few around," the man told him. "Found this one in West Virginia. She needed a new gyrounit, but she's fine now."

"Tell Jonath how grateful I am," said Logan.

"He'll be glad to hear you're all right."

*Thanks to you,* Logan thought, looking at Dia.

And she smiled at him.

"Will you be following me back?" the man asked Logan.

*No. We're going west. Together.*

"No," said Logan. "We'll be going west."

The two men shook hands. "Good trip," said Logan.

With Dia, he watched the ship fade into night sky.

*Where now?* asked Logan. *How far west?*

*All the way to the Coast,* she told him, sitting beside him in the humming paravane. The New York Territory unrolled below them, nightblack and massive.

*I want to take you home, Logan.* She smiled, her hands touching gently at the planes of his face. *West, to my home.*

As heat is felt on skin, Logan felt the passion radiating from her mind.

He owed her his life, but could he give her something more than gratitude? Was he capable, now, of a greater commitment to her?

Logan wasn't sure.

He would know when the time for knowing was at hand.

# EYES

Liath was waiting for them on the shore.

Before he saw her, Logan received her warm thoughts, reaching into the sky to greet him: *Welcome, Logan . . . Welcome to our home!*

The paravane, sweeping over her, whipped Liath's long hair in a silver halo around her delicately-sculptured face and neck. The smokegown she wore billowed up in a swirl of mistsilks, revealing a lithe, cat-muscled body. She waved happily at them.

*Is she not beautiful?*

*Yes—as you are, Dia.*

Logan set down in the sand at the ocean's edge. The Pacific lifted sleeves of bluegreen lace and spilled them at their feet as Dia and Logan climbed free of the ship.

The two sisters embraced, holding one another tightly.

There was no hesitation in their movements, no blind fumbling—yet they were sightless!

*No, we see, Logan.*

*And with a clairty much greater than yours.*

*You steal my thoughts!*

Both girls smiled, a double radiance. It was early morning and the sun made a bronze shield of the ocean; the sky was newly-washed with wind, and flowed like another ironblue sea, free of clouds, to the horizon. The sharp odors of brine and kelp reached Logan, mixed with the cry of an overhead gull, circling and curious.

Liath took Logan's hand. *I am glad you are safe,* she told him.

*Your sister . . . She reached me when no one else could.*

They walked along the wet sand.

Dia took Logan's other hand, and the sisters guided him inland, toward a rising cliff of pink coral.

*Our home,* nodded Dia.

*Our castle!* enthused Liath.

It was literally that: an immense castle of fibrous pink-and-white coral rising sheer from the sand. Sun spangled its daggered edges.

*Careful . . . Walk where we walk,* warned Dia. *The coral is very sharp.*

Logan followed them along a path of beaten stone which wound up into the depths of the structure.

They emerged, finally, into a wide, sun-splashed chamber, lined with thick, tufted flowcloth. Here every coral edge was softened by resilient layers of cloth, by pillowrugs and foamcushions.

*Watch!*

Delightedly, Liath skipped across the room to a large, coral-crystal pillar. She placed her hand on the pillar and, slowly, a series of silver curtains hushed down from the ceiling, forming a protective tenting over their heads.

*These are weather shells,* Dia told him. *We are not like father. Our skin grows cold at night. They protect us from wind and fog.*

*And for warmth . . .* said Liath.

She pressed another section of crystal—and a fire bloomed to life in the center of the floor.

*Incredible.*

*We want you to live here with us, Logan,* Dia told him. *Share our home, our lives . . . our love.*

Liath's thoughts flowed in: *There are just the two of us. One is nearly always with father at the Bridge. We alternate.*

*When Liath is gone, it can be lonely . . .*

*For me, also, when Dia is away . . . We need you, Logan.*

*Need you . . .*

*A pairbond?* questioned Logan. *Between all three of us?*

*It could be beautiful, Logan!*

And Logan thought: *Jaq is gone.*

*Gone,* they echoed.

*Jess is gone.*

*Gone . . .* mind-whispered Dia.

*And we are here,* said Liath.

A night. A day. Another night . . .

Logan found joy with Dia and Liath. Their minds and bodies rioted together in a spillout of sensual delights, a crossfire of thoughts, emotions, impressions, shared experiences . . .

But there was a barrier.

*Your eyes, Logan. They blind you to sight.*

Dia was with him. They were lazing nude in the slow ocean tides along a sun-tinted stretch of yellow beach.

Logan smiled. *I see the sun on the water. I see gulls in the sky . . .* He touched her body. *I see your beauty . . .*

*But I see more,* she told him. *So much more, Logan! My vision is achieved with the inner eye, and is on a scale beyond your conception. Whole worlds are open to me which are closed to you. I want to share them.*

*How?*

*You must free your inner eye—allow it to expand your total consciousness.*

*For me, Dia, that's impossible.*

*No, you're wrong. You need only remove the barrier of your outer sight to free that greater sight which is within you. It waits to be released.*

*Are you saying that I should—blind myself?*

She shook her head, smiling softly. *No, I'm saying you should free yourself . . . enter our world . . . Liath's and mine. Become truly bonded to us. You have the ability as few others have it. As we are gifted, so are you.*

*And how would I do this?*

*There is a heat shield in the castle . . . of sunmetal. Its surface is as bright as the sun itself. Stand before it, gaze full into it with your physical eyes—and it will free you. It will take away the barrier which separates us.*

*Is it really possible?*

*It is, Logan, it is!*

That night, in the castle, Logan could not sleep.

Existence had no reality, now, beyond the daughters of Andar. Dia had saved him from certain death and, in a way, his life was hers.

She had asked nothing of him; she had only given. Now she wanted to give more . . . wanted to give him her inner world, share it with him.

Why was he so afraid of losing his eyes? He had seen the cities, the cruelty, the terror and frenzy of runners fleeing the Gun. He had seen the plague run its terrible path across Argos, destroying his friends, all the people he had come to know and trust. He'd seen the Wilderness People, lost and helpless against the ravages of nature. He'd seen his son's sprawled body . . .

Jaq was dead. Jessica was dead. What more was there for him, in this world of shadows?

Noon. The sun tall and direct above the castle. The three of them standing before a high, curtained object.

*When we move aside the curtain, look full into the shield,* Dia told him. *Do not blink or shift your gaze.*

*For ten seconds. That's all it will require,* assured

Liath. *There will be no pain—only an intense brightness.*

*I understand.*

Dia embraced him, kissed his lips. *Trust us, Logan.*

*I do. I trust you both.*

*Ten seconds—and you will be with us forever,* said Liath.

Logan braced himself, teeth clamped, jaw muscles tight. He nodded.

*Open the curtain!*

Dia moved to the shield, drew back its wine-red cover.

Brightness! Incredible, penetrating brightness . . . a sun-glare of fierce light so intense that Logan flinched back from it.

Yet, he did not blink.

*Six seconds!*

*Seven . . .*

*Three more seconds, Logan!*

A rush of sound above them. Blades chopping air. The red curtain swirled, lifted itself, settled to half-cover the shield.

Logan turned away to a wild cry from above: "Logan! Quick, Logan! I have news!"

The voice of Jonath.

In a fantail of sand, the paravane came to rest on the beach. Jonath leaped from the machine, ran toward Logan, waving, shouting.

They met at the coral's edge.

"I flew here the moment I heard the news. I would allow no one else to bring it."

"*What* news, Jonath?"

The Wilderness leader gripped his friend by both shoulders; his eyes blazed with the words: "She's alive! Jessica's *alive!*"

# JONATH

"All right, tell me *everything* you know," Logan said tightly.

They were in the castle. Jonath was seated on a fall of snowpillows, sipping green seawine which Dia had brought him. She and her sister hovered near Logan, who was never entirely still. He paced constantly as he listened to Jonath, questioned him on details.

"An ex-Sandman named Evans brought me the news," said the Wilderness man. "He told me—"

"Evans 9?"

"Yes," said Jonath.

"I've known him since childhood. We worked the Angeles Complex together."

Jonath nodded. "He *said* he was your friend—that he'd become a runner because of you."

"Evans . . . running?"

"You made it to Sanctuary and so he decided to try for it—but he couldn't connect with Ballard's people. Evans was hiding out when they penetrated the Line at Steinbeck."

"Why would he tie in with Gant?"

"After the Thinker died he told me he just naturally gravitated back with other ex-Sandmen. When Gant took command of their group Evans followed along."

A flash of instant mental communication between Logan and the sisters: *Who is Gant?*

*A monster. The worst of the Sandmen. He hates me.*

*Why?*

*He was in charge of Angeles Complex when I became a runner. My escape to Sanctuary was a per-*

*sonal embarrassment to him, a black mark on his record. I was the only Sandman to ever reach Sanctuary, and he hates me for it.*

"Evans and Gant argued," said Jonath. "Gant tried to have him killed. He got away, came to us, looking for you. He wanted you to know that Gant bought Jessica on the Market."

"That Borgia bitch lied to me," said Logan. "She had me convinced that Jess was dead."

"To protect herself, obviously," said Jonath. "By shifting the blame to Prince, she thought you'd let her go."

"But I didn't," said Logan flatly.

Dia looked agonized. *You're leaving us! Your thoughts say it.*

*I'm going after Jess.*

*But Gant—he'll never let you have her.*

*I'll take her.*

*He'll kill you, Logan!*

*He'll probably try.*

*The Sandmen are with him. You'll never—*

"Where is she?" Logan asked Jonath. A muscle danced in his cheek. "Where does Gant have her?"

Jonath told him.

## DAKOTAS

Deep green below them. A forest flow of pine-thick wilderness, broken by high granite cliffs and jeweled lakes, darkened by the swift-sliding shadow of the paravane.

The Black Hills of the Dakotas.

"When we get there," Logan said, "I want you to stay with the ship until I bring Jess out."

"Negative. I'm going in with you," said Jonath. "You'll need all the help you can get."

"Then take one of these." He handed Jonath a Fuser. "Courtesy of the Borgias."

"I've never fired one."

"Nothing to it. Just aim—and press the gripstud with your thumb. It's laser-powered. The beam will cut through any surface."

"Do you think we've actually got a chance of bringing her out?"

"Would it make any difference if I said no?"

Jonath sighed, idly turning the weapon in his hand. "The fact that you know he's got her . . . that dictates your action."

"But not yours," said Logan. "Why *did* you come with me, Jonath?"

"Because you're my friend." He smiled. "And I happen to place a high value on friendship. It's one of the few real things I can count on in this brave new world of ours."

"Did Evans tell you how many Sandmen Gant has with him?"

"At least two dozen . . . maybe more. He wasn't sure."

"It's Gant himself I worry about," said Logan. "The man's a total fighting machine. And he doesn't make mistakes."

"Evans told me Gant thinks you're dead, that the Borgias killed you at Steinbeck."

"Good. That means he won't be expecting our visit. Gives us a slight edge going in."

They rode in silence above the Dakotas.

Logan thought of Liath, and of Dia. Of ocean sunsets and midnight sands and clean sea air—and of lying with them in soft coral darkness . . . They knew he'd never return to them. And when he left they'd sent their farewells soaring after him as the paravane lifted away from the beach . . .

*We love you, Logan! . . . We'll always love you.*
*Always.*
*Always.*
Fading. Dying out behind him . . .
*Always.*
*Always.*
*Always.*

"There!" Jonath pointed excitedly downward. "Rushmore! We're close now."

The rippling shadow of the paravane flowed over the somber granite heads of Mount Rushmore.

Logan took precautions: Gant might have posted a lookout, and since surprise was essential he brought the paravane down in a tree-screened ravine well short of their goal.

"Last chance to change your mind," Logan said as the blades idled to silence.

"Let's go," said Jonath, his mouth set in a stubborn line.

"If we move fast enough," said Logan, "we should be able to get there by sundown."

He stowed the Fuser in his belt and removed a canister of water from the paravane.

"We should cover the ship," said Jonath. "If we make it back here and it's gone . . ."

"No one can spot it from the air," Logan assured him. "Not down in this ravine. It's safe enough."

And they set off.

The country was extremely rugged, laced with drifts of sharp rock and tangled root-grass which slowed their progress. Brambles tore at their skin; sun hammered their backs.

At a rest halt Logan shared the canister of water with his friend.

"How much farther?" asked the Wilderness leader, breathing heavily, his back against a pine.

"Hour maybe," said Logan. "When I was here before, with Jess, I came in from another direction. But we should sight it soon."

They did.

The pride of the Dakotas.

A carved granite mammoth rising for more than five hundred and fifty feet into the sky of the Black Hills.

A warrior chief riding a mighty stallion.

A mountain that had become a man: Crazy Horse.

They were standing on a high ridge with a clear view of the mountain.

"Magnificent!" declared Jonath, staring at the awesome figure.

"He led the Sioux against Custer at Little Big Horn," said Logan. "Tashunca-uitco. A great leader. They say his arm points toward the Happy Hunting Ground of his people."

"And now he belongs to Gant," said Jonath bitterly.

They started down the ridge.

The sun had tipped to the western horizon when they reached the base of Crazy Horse.

Logan raised a hand, hesitating. A gold object glittered in deep grass to his left.

Something alive? A hidden Sandman?

He moved cautiously toward it, weapon in hand, Jonath following.

A glazed ruby eye stared up at Logan; its lens was shattered; part of a broken, rusting bulk of sunken metal.

"What is it?"

"Mech eagle," said Logan, leaning to examine the ruptured metal corpse. "Robot guardian designed to protect Crazy Horse. Looks like this one died with the Thinker."

Jonath picked up a portion of bronzed wingfeather. "Big," he said.

"And deadly," said Logan. "A pair of them ripped me last time I came here." Logan pointed upward, to the head of the warrior. "They lived on his shoulders. Went after anything that moved."

"Then let's be glad this one's not active."

Logan smiled.

"How do we get inside?" asked Jonath.

"There are three main access caves, but Gant would likely have men at each . . . Our best bet is to get in from above. Through a break in the rock."

"I'm not much good at climbing," Jonath said.

"We won't need to go too high," Logan told him. "Mountain's split in several places. Just a matter of picking one."

Logan reconnoitered the flank of rising rock, climbing up to investigate two of the cave-like surface splits. Satisfied, he gestured to Jonath.

"Here," he said. "This one."

Awkwardly, Jonath climbed up to join him.

"Be extremely careful inside," Logan warned. "One loose rock could fall all the way to the bottom. Our game would be up."

Jonath nodded.

Logan removed a small bulletlight from his tunic. "I'll have to keep this shielded," he said, "but at least we won't be in total darkness. Stay behind me."

"I sure don't plan to lead," smiled Jonath.

"One thing puzzles me," said Logan.

"What?"

"Why didn't Evans supply you with information on *where* Gant has Jessica? We could blunder around for *miles* in there!"

"My fault, really," admitted Jonath. "When he told me she was alive I was so anxious to reach you with the news that I failed to question him fully."

"Doesn't matter," said Logan. "If Jess is alive in

there I'll find her . . . no matter how far we go or how long it takes."

## THINKER

They had agreed to converse only out of necessity once they were inside the mountain—and now they moved in silence between pressing walls of deep-winding rock. Downward.

Toward the Thinker.

Built in the 1980s on a massive research grant, and symbolizing one of the high points of human scientific achievement, it had never been designed to rule Earth. Its final installation here, in the Crazy Horse caverns in 1991, opened a whole new research era, promising an end to disease and poverty. The truly immense computer-complex, with its mechanical cells numbering ten raised to the seventeenth power, was a natural extension of the space-probe computers of the 1970s, but with much vaster potential.

Until the Little War.

When the young took charge of world government, they also took over the Thinker—re-programming it to their own ends, setting up the Death-at-21 society with this supreme god-computer as their major arm of enforcement. The cities of Earth lived in its metallic grip, becoming totally dependent upon it. The Thinker's multi-million arteries became the world's prime root system, feeding power and control to each city around the globe.

As knight slays dragon, Ballard had killed the computer. It lay now, acres of blackened, inert metal, an endless cemetery of silent relays and ruptured cables, stretching for becalmed miles beneath the granite bulk of Crazy Horse.

But even in death, the Thinker inspired awe.

"It was alive when I was here with Jess," said Logan softly, as he and Jonath stood on a wide ledge overlooking the complex. Fissured cracks in the rock walls of the mountain allowed thin spears of light to cut across the vast, dead-metal plain of linked computer banks.

"It goes on forever!" marveled Jonath. He started moving toward the floor of the caverns. Logan caught him just before his foot touched the dust-dulled surface, pulled him back abruptly.

"What's wrong? Gant isn't in this section."

"Not Gant," said Logan. "The Watchman."

"Watchman?"

"Another robot kill-device. Programmed to react instantly to the slightest pressure on the floor's surface." Logan picked up a small pebble, tossed it onto the flooring.

Silence. No alarms. No movement.

"We're all right," sighed Logan. "It's dead." He grinned at Jonath. "Believe me, you don't want that thing coming after you."

"Which way now?" asked Jonath.

"I'm not sure," said Logan, looking down a long row of silent computer banks. "Did Evans say why Gant picked Crazy Horse as his headquarters?"

"No. Just that he was here."

"He's probably rigged up some kind of auxiliary power—for light and heat. Using parts of the Thinker. Once we locate the power source we've found Gant."

"This thing spreads out for miles."

"Best chance is to head for the Central Core. Gant could have tapped into it for his power. If so, his headquarters will be close to the Core."

"But I thought this was dead . . . *all* of it."

"The components still exist," said Logan. "Gant might have found a way to partially reactivate some of them." He took out the canister of water, opened it. "Want some?"

"My throat's been dry ever since we got here," admitted Jonath, taking several swallows.

Logan drank, then stowed the canister back in his tunic. "Let's go. And walk softly *all* the way."

Weapons in hand, they headed for the Core.

## ALIVE

Theoretically, Logan knew where the heart of the Thinker was located, but he'd never seen it. However, if his reasoning was correct regarding Gant's use of this potential power center, the Core would soon reveal itself.

A hive-hum of energy alerted them as they moved down one of the mile-long corridors. A golden wash of light haloed the darkness ahead of them.

Logan spoke in a low whisper to Jonath: "Gant's men could be anywhere in this area. Keep close to the banks."

The sound increased.

"Crawl," directed Logan, dropping to his stomach. "We're almost there."

They inched forward, emerging onto a spiral of balcony which overlooked the glowing mass of the Central Core.

It was huge—an interlinking of incredibly-complex electronic columns, rising into the upper level of the mountain, each golden column pulsing with incalculable energies. At least half of the columns were "alive."

Logan was stunned. The display of computer power

astonished him. In reactivating this much of the Core Gant had accomplished far more than Logan had believed possible.

To what purpose? Surely he had harnessed considerably more power than his personal use required.

"I want to get closer," Logan told Jonath. "You stay here while I—"

"Closer?" an amplified voice boomed and crashed around them. "A simple wish, Logan 3. One that I shall be happy to grant."

A cluster of pinbeams raked the balcony as Logan and Jonath sprang back, guns ready.

Logan blinked into the glare: "Are you Gant?"

"I am," the voice crackled.

"Where's Jessica?"

"Where indeed!" And the voice boomed in laughter. "Why should I tell you anything?"

"We're armed," Logan warned. "We can do a lot of damage here."

A dark figure advanced on them along the curving balcony. "That's an empty threat," said a voice that Logan recognized immediately.

"Evans!"

"Been a long time, Logan. When you made it to Argos I thought we'd never see you again. Yet . . ." And he smiled. "Here you are!"

Jonath was trembling with rage. "You *used* me—to get Logan here. Everything you told me . . . lies! All lies!"

"Not everything," said Evans smoothly, covering them with his Gun. "I said that Gant was here, which he is. And that he'd taken Jessica. Also true."

Jonath's eyes blazed. He raised the Fuser. "You filthy—"

Evans Gunned him. Ripper. In a sudden eruption of heat Jonath's body was blown apart. The remains of his charred corpse sprawled at Logan's feet.

"You are surrounded, Logan," boomed Gant's

voice. "My men have been pacing you since the moment you entered Crazy Horse. Now, if you wish to see Jessica alive you'll hand your weapon to Evans 9."

"Do it," snapped Evans.

Face tight, eyes hard on his ex-friend, Logan handed the Fuser to Evans.

Other Sandmen materialized around him. One of them tapewired Logan's hands behind his back; another quickly looped a chokechain around his neck, affixed it to his wrists, snugged it tight.

During this, Logan remained silent.

With a tight smile, Evans said, "Welcome back, friend."

Logan spat in his face.

## GANT

Seven feet tall. Bare-waisted. Dark, burnished skin. Deep-sunk, luminous eyes. A shark's slash of mouth.

Gant.

Logan stood before him, flanked by two Sandmen.

"Down," said Gant to one of them.

In response, the Sandman jerked fiercely on Logan's chokechain, forcing him to his knees.

Gant walked around him in a slow circle. "Your body's in good condition." He prodded Logan's shoulder. "Solid muscle tone. I'm happy to see that you've maintained yourself. So many ex-Sandmen go slack, allow their bodies to—"

*"Where—is—she?"* Logan's voice was edged, the words spaced with cold anger.

"You'll see her," said Gant. "I give you my absolute promise that the two of you shall soon be reunited."

"Have you . . . harmed her?"

Gant looked down at Logan and, for the first time, smiled at him. The smile was grotesque. The tall man had replaced his teeth with rubies. They glittered like blood in Gant's wide jaw.

"I never harm a thing of value," he said. "And Jessica has been of immense value to me." Again the jeweled smile. "She brought me *you.*"

He gestured to the Sandmen. Logan was dragged up, pushed into a couch facing Gant's desk.

The tall man eased into a lifeleather chair, folded his hands and leaned across the mirrored expanse of desk. "This mountain is mine, Logan. It was Ballard's once. But he got careless."

Logan found it all but impossible to listen to Gant, talk to him with any degree of calm; he wanted, with every ounce of his conscious being, to launch himself at the man's throat.

"You smashed the Sanctuary Line at Steinbeck," said Logan. ". . . and followed Ballard here."

"That's correct. But I was a bit late in arriving. Before I killed him Ballard had time to destroy a large part of the Thinker. Fortunately, not all. As you can see, he left the greater part of the Core intact."

Logan remained silent as Gant fingered a large, square-cut ruby, one of several on the desk. He studied his captive, turning the ruby slowly in his fingers. "Now I have the Central Core, and you. A double bonus."

"All these years . . . you've been brooding about my escape."

"You dishonored me as a Sandman!"

"You *have* no honor, Gant! You've *never* had it. All you're after is revenge."

"An honorable goal in itself," said Gant. "Many great men have sought it." He chuckled. "In fact, when you killed at Steinbeck you were seeking exactly *that* against the Borgias. Revenge."

"I wanted Jess back. I went there to find her—but it was you behind it all. *You* had her taken!"

"No, I'm afraid I can't claim credit for that. The outlanders happened upon her, didn't realize the prize they'd found. I was able to purchase her for a very modest price. But the price didn't matter . . ."

He stood up, walked casually over to Logan, buried his right fist in his hair and savagely jerked Logan's head back. "I wanted you, Logan." His voice was cold iron. "Wanted you *here!*"

Then he smiled again, releasing his grip, moved back to his desk. "Actually, until Jessica was put on the Market, I was not aware that you'd returned to Earth. But once I found her it made everything simple. Buy her. Hold her. Get word to you. Wait for you. All very simple."

"How do I know you haven't killed her?"

"You don't," said Gant. "I thought carefully about it, thought about bringing you here and showing you her corpse . . . but decided on a richer plan. One that will . . . *satisfy* me more."

"Were you . . . satisfied with Jonath's death?" asked Logan bitterly.

"He was brandishing a weapon. There was no other course of action possible."

"Look . . ." Logan drew in a breath. "We've *had* our talk. When do I see Jess?"

"Soon. As I promised," smiled the tall man. "I note, by the way, that you seem to find my smile unusual. Rubies happen to be a personal vanity of mine. I visited a New You and had these put in. I rather *like* the effect."

"Why can't I see Jessica now?"

Gant's face tightened. "Because I say you can't. First . . . there's a special room you must visit. Of my own design. I think you'll find it . . . stimulating. *After* your visit there you'll be reunited with Jessica."

"If you're lying to me, Gant . . . If she's dead . . ."

"What will you do?"

"I'll kill you. Somehow, I'll *kill* you."

Gant laughed, a booming sound in the room. "As a Sandman you never lacked bravado, Logan. Always full of drive, self-confidence . . . But, in your present situation, threatening me is an empty and ridiculous gesture." He took a Fuser from his desk, moved quickly to press the flanged barrel against Logan's forehead. "I could burn you in an instant."

"I don't deny it," said Logan. His eyes met Gant's, locked on them. "But you heard what I said."

Gant flung aside the weapon, abruptly turned his bronzed back on Logan. He raised a hand. "Take him away."

And Logan was dragged from the room.

## STORM

In the six years since the death of the cities Gant had built his personal kingdom at Crazy Horse. Stripping the Thinker itself for raw materials, he'd constructed a miniature city beneath the mountain. Logan saw only parts of it as they marched him down hallways, past labs and crew quarters, through a courtyard, past food-storage lockers . . . but he was impressed.

Yet he did not ask questions. His curiosity about Gant was canceled by his consuming desire to see Jessica, to hold her again . . . She's here, he told himself, *here* in one of these buildings . . .

Escape, at this point, was a useless hope. In addition to the chokechain and tapewire, the four Sandmen who walked with him (one leading, one to either side, another following) all carried Guns in their hands.

He would do as they instructed. If Gant had not

been lying, he'd be allowed to see Jess after whatever torture the man had set up for him to endure. And Logan had endured much in his life. He would endure this—and hope.

*Jess, Jess . . . I love you!*

"Stop here," said the lead Sandman.

They had reached a wide duralloy door, set flush into the corridor's end. The door was solid metal, and smelled of oil. One of the Sandmen unlocked it, swung it back. "Inside," he said.

Logan entered—and the heavy door crashed shut behind him.

Soft laughter in the corridor, and the Sandmen were gone.

Logan was alone.

The chamber was large, perhaps twenty by twenty feet, of bolted metal, totally bare. Not a single item of any kind—just metal walls, ceiling, floor. And, as Logan tested the surface, cool to the touch.

There were round holes of varying size punched into the ceiling, scores of them. And as many in the floor. The walls were vented, top to bottom.

Am I to be gassed in here? Is that Gant's plan? Ironic. Saved in New York from the same fate I'll suffer here . . . Will Gant really allow me to see Jess?

Will I leave this room alive?

Logan raised his head, tensing his body; he swung around abruptly.

*Someone was touching him!*

No, not someone. Something: a slight draft of currented air, touching at his face, his hair . . . emanating from the vents. Fresh. Not gas. Fresh air.

But subtly increasing, gradually becoming stronger.

A soft, pattering sound—and Logan felt wetness against his skin. Slow drops of water, dripping down on him from a multitude of ceiling holes.

A muted rumble from the room, a faint, far-distant sound, like the throb of giant drums.

The current of air had become a breeze, blowing chill against Logan's rapidly-dampening uniform. The patter of drops from the ceiling intensified, became a steady downfall, soaking Logan's hair and clothing.

The breeze soon mounted to a *wind,* whipping at Logan in cold gusts from the wallvents surrounding him.

The downpour increased to a fierce curtain of iced sleet, and the muted drum-rumble boomed into full thunder, assaulting Logan's eardrums.

He staggered back, dazed, helpless—as the wind punished him, building in force by the second.

Now another frightening element manifested itself in the chamber: firebolts of lightning danced and crackled around him, first at one wall, then at the next.

Logan clapped both hands to his ears to muffle the thunder's brutal roar, his mouth gaping in shocked agony.

A solid gust of wind slapped him to the floor. He rose to his knees, fighting for balance on the rainslick metal, crawled toward a corner to lessen the storm's impact—but a sizzle of heat-lightning forced him back to the room's center.

The wind was a demon's shriek, the thunderclaps now impossibly loud in the metal chamber.

Something began cutting at Logan's skin, drawing blood along his cheek. Hailstones—sharp-edged pellets of cold ice which pounded and slashed at his unprotected head and shoulders.

Now the wind suddenly reversed direction, taking Logan by surprise; under its gale force, he was toppled and slammed into the wall.

Again the hurricane blast abruptly reversed direction, and Logan was hurled across the slippery floor into the opposite wall, striking the metal with bone-crushing impact.

Again.

And again.

And again.

Viciously pelted and buffeted, Logan lay gasping on his back, blood running from a dozen wounds, the hail and rain drumming his flesh.

He opened his mouth and cried out, but his voice was swallowed up in the cruel, unending din.

As the storm raged.

## REUNION

"Do you think he's ready now?" asked Evans 9.

Gant nodded. "Tell them to kill the storm, then have Logan brought to Room K . . ." His smile glowed red. ". . . where I shall keep my promise to him."

Evans turned to leave when Gant's voice stopped him.

"One thing I'd like to know."

"Yes?"

"I'm curious," said Gant. "What made you betray him? You were friends once . . . yet you set the trap that brought him here."

"I'm a proud man," said Evans. "Logan kept me in his shadow. In DS he assumed a position of superiority. He was arrogant, self-serving. He never tried to understand me. Even took our friendship for granted. Thought it was a privilege for me to be his friend! But I was *never* his friend! I knew someday I'd best him. And I have."

"Indeed you have," nodded Gant. "It seems we share similar emotional attitudes toward Logan. Which helps bind us in the venture."

"I want him dead," said Evans flatly.

And he left.

When they opened the door Logan did not move, did not look at them. Water dripped languorously from the ceiling, draining away along the floor.

The storm was over.

Logan lay in a far corner of the chamber, knees drawn up tight against his body, head sunken against his chest, eyes closed. His breathing was irregular. His soaked, torn uniform was spotted with blood.

Two Sandmen walked over to him, lifted him by the elbows, dragging him toward the door. He moved in a broken child's stumble, his eyes glazed, unfocused. Small, mewling sounds issued from his mouth.

The Sandmen smiled at one another as they led him away from the stormroom.

Room K formed part of Gant's personal living quarters, and was lavish. Cut from the natural rock of the mountain, it was walled in leathertrim and lit by moonglobes, which cast their soft radiance on Jessica's pale skin. When Gant entered she rushed to him, eyes pleading. "Have you brought Logan? Where is he?"

Gant ran a dark hand along the shine of her hair. "They're bringing him. He'll be here *soon,* I assure you."

She turned away, slipped nervously into a bodychair. The green silk gown she wore, cut low at the breasts, pressed in against the curves of her body.

"I'm sure he'll find you as desirable as ever," Gant said, moving to a winetable. Seating himself, he sampled a French vintage, inhaling its subtle bouquet. "The Borgias treated you well, all things considered. They could have disfigured you, ruined your beauty."

"They were *foul* to me," she said.

"Come now, Jessica. Put yourself in their place.

You belonged to them. You were a woman of strong sexual attraction. Naturally they—used you. But Lucrezia knew enough not to allow abuse. That was the key. She kept your Market value intact." He chuckled. "Had she known just how much I wanted you, and for what ultimate purpose, she could have realized a much greater profit."

"I'm glad Logan killed her," said Jessica darkly. "She didn't deserve to live—not after what she did to Jaq."

"Your Logan is a strong-willed, violent man." He hesitated, for effect. "Or should I say . . . *was.*"

Jessica looked startled, suddenly frightened. Her eyes sought Gant's. "Then, he's *not* coming! You've lied to me . . . Logan is dead!"

Gant smiled, and the moonglobes flashed crimson from his rubied teeth. "No, not dead. Merely . . . gentled . . . eased from his violence. I have given him the gift of bodily peace."

"Why should I believe anything you say?"

"I went to a great deal of trouble to have him brought here to you. In justice, you should be *grateful* to me, not suspicious."

Jessica's eyes burned with heat; her hands were fisted. "You hate us both for daring to do what you lacked the courage to do—for seeking Sanctuary."

"I stood by my duty," said Gant, his voice gone hard. "Logan ran from his."

The door chimed softly.

"Ah, the moment of your reconciliation is at hand," said Gant. "It should be touching." He palmed the door and it whispered open.

Logan was there, his sagging body held erect between two Sandmen. He blinked rapidly as Jessica ran forward to embrace him.

"Logan . . . oh, *Logan!*" She put her arms around him, frantically kissed his lips, held his face between her cupped hands. He showed no sign of recognition.

His face was totally expressionless.

"He doesn't know me!" She swung toward Gant, stunned. "What have you *done* to him?"

Gant smiled, a red gash of pleasure.

Logan stared at nothing.

## FRIEND

They were stripped naked and thrown into a cell of raw rock, dirt-floored, exposed to constant drafts of cold air slicing through the interior of Crazy Horse. Gant's instructions were concise: No clothing. No food. Water at two-day intervals.

He wanted to see them rot.

Logan was helpless. He whimpered, lacked control of his body functions, was incapable of speech. As Jessica held him, his muscles jerked spastically. His eyes rolled white. Saliva dribbled from the corners of his slack mouth.

The stormroom had broken him.

Through the long hours, Jessica crooned to him, stroked his trembling skin with gentle fingers—but he did not know her. She was a warm presence, nothing more, in the dim gray web of his mental world.

Her voice was a litany: "Logan, my darling . . . my dearest . . . Logan . . . Logan . . . Logan, my love . . .

But they had a friend at Crazy Horse—a silent figure weaving in shadowed stealth through the twisting rock caverns surrounding the Thinker—a friend who knew Gant's ways and awaited the chance to move against him.

Watching.

Waiting.

Until a plan was evolved.
And acted upon.

Gant entered their cell with Steratt, his chief guard. Steratt was lean and sharp-featured, with the muscles of a hunting dog; he was dressed in slash-chest ivory leathers, wore thighboots and carried a small black handcase.

Jessica looked up at them, blinking, nestling Logan close to her shoulder.

Gant opened the handcase, took out a looped object.

Bodywhip.

He handed the whip to Jessica. "Use it on him," he said in a flat, emotionless tone.

"No!" She threw it aside.

Gant nodded to Steratt. He pulled Jessica up by her hair, swinging her toward Gant. Who slapped her. Hard.

Logan blinked at them, his face devoid of expression.

Blood flecked Jessica's mouth. "I . . . *won't,*" she gasped.

"If you don't," said Gant, taking a Fuser from his belt, aiming it at Logan, "I'll burn him where he lies!"

Logan blinked stupidly.

"Pick it up," said Gant, "and use it now." His eyes blazed black.

Jessica picked up the whip.

Behind the Medsupply Unit, in caverned rock darkness, a shape moved.

The Sandman in charge of guarding the unit was bored. He was thinking how much better the workers' guard had it—with females to use whenever he felt the urge. Just go into the cells, drag one out, use her and toss her back inside. The workers didn't complain. Who would they complain to? Oh, they didn't *like* it. One of them tried to club a guard once, while he was busy with a female, but they burned him. As an example. It didn't pay to attack a guard. They all realized that.

Well, Steratt owed him a shift change. He'd been on Med now for a month. Maybe he could get switched to Workers next. End up with some nice young meat.

The shape detached itself from the rocks, moved closer.

The Sandman yawned, sat down, arms folded across his chest. He closed his eyes and thought about women . . .

While the shadow-figure darted into the unit, unseen.

Hypokit. Fresh needles. Healpacs. Wraps and cotton.

Careful! Arrange the other supplies to cover what's taken. No breakage. No noise. Quickly . . . quickly!

And a shadow drifted back into the caverns.

Imprisoned inside the mountain, Jessica had lost all sense of time. As she held her man, this brave human who had given his selfhood to save her, she felt they'd been like this, together in Gant's cell, for many months. . . . Sometimes, her mind, disoriented by lack of food, held the conviction that they would be here forever, immortal in agony, abandoned, unfed, their bodies racked by cold, thinned by hunger . . .

Then Gant would come. To gloat. To enjoy the spectacle. Sometimes she would be given to Evans or Steratt, who would take her brutally in the cell, for Gant's amusement. But, mostly, it was darkness, cold, hard dirt against aching muscles, night-crawling insects . . .

Logan never spoke. He lay in her arms, unable to relate to her, to his bleak surroundings, to hunger or pain.

Yet Jessica loved him more fiercely than ever.

And, until Gant killed them, her love for Logan would remain—a hard, unwavering flame that warmed the deepest part of her.

She would endure.

*They* would endure.

Assigned to Logan's cell unit, in six-hour shifts: eight Sandmen, two of them always on guard. Top men. Personally selected by Gant.

On this shift: Lister 4 and Brun 11. Humorless, hard-faced, alert as cats. They paced outside the unit, carrying (at Gant's direct order) Guns in their hands.

"Had a runner once," Lister was saying, in a tight, controlled voice, "who got into a Nursery. Got past the robots. I had to go in after him."

"And?" said Brun.

"Had him backed to the wall in a Cribroom. I was ready to homer him, when this Autogoverness comes rolling in. Upset. Won't let me fire. All worried about the infants. She knocks the Gun out of my hand. Runner makes a dive for it. Gets his hand around it. *Zip!* Blows his arm off to the shoulder!"

"Runners know better," said Brun.

"Guess this one forgot," said Lister, a faint smile tracing his lips. "Anyway, when I—"

Lister stopped, the smile vanishing. He sat down very slowly, then toppled sideways, laying his face into the dirt.

A small, glinting hyponeedle projected from his neck.

Brun wheeled in a covering arc, Gun up, peering into the cave-darkness around him.

No sound.

No movement.

He was about to press the alarmstud just inside the unit's arched doorway when a second needle sang from blackness, deeply imbedding itself in his carotid artery.

The Gun slipped from Brun's nerveless fingers as he sank to his knees. His eyes lost focus. He collapsed backward, head striking the edge of the rock doorway—but he did not feel the impact.

Silence.

Then—a soft scratch of loose pebbles.

A shape, moving.

Jessica saw the figure coming swiftly down the gloomed corridor toward their cell. Not Gant. Or Evans. Or Steratt. Or the guards.

*Who then?*

An assassin sent to kill them?

No, Gant had vowed he'd be there personally to watch them die, and Jessica knew that was one promise he would keep.

"I'm Mary-Mary 2," the figure said. "You met me once, long ago."

Jessica looked at the girl. Slim. Intense. Dressed in a ripped green tunicdress. And didn't know her.

Mary-Mary smiled. "In the Angeles Complex. Under Cathedral. I was only five then. I'd escaped Nursery."

"Yes," said Jessica. "Now I remember. But how did you ever—"

"No questions," said Mary-Mary. "I got rid of both guards, but there's very little time." She produced a ridged silver key, hurriedly opened their cell door with it.

The chamber smelled of damp earth and rock mold, a fungoid odor of decay.

"He can't walk," said Jessica, looking down at Logan who was curled into a ball in the center of the dirt floor, arms clasping his updrawn legs. His eyes were open. He was staring at the wall.

"Together we can manage him," said Mary-Mary. "I'm stronger than I look."

The women half-lifted, half-dragged Logan to a standing position. His head rolled on his neck; a bubble of saliva formed and broke on his paste-white lips.

A clang of distant metal. Door being opened, closed.

"Hurry!" urged Mary-Mary. "Someone's coming."

## SEARCH

Gant. Evans. Steratt. Joking about what they would find in the cell ahead of them. Laughing, as they moved down the corridor.

Suddenly, an oath from Gant. "Gone!" he thundered. "Their cell's empty!"

"Someone used a key," said Evans. "The door wasn't forced."

Gant was wearing a large ruby ring with a chased-silver facing on the index finger on his right hand. The ring opened the side of Steratt's face under Gant's blow. "You! You're in charge of the cells! You're responsible!"

"They can't be far away," said Evans. He was kneeling in the cell, one hand to the floor. "Still warm from their bodies."

Gant turned from Steratt, who was groaning, half-conscious. "Maximum alert. Have the outside of the mountain completely sealed off. They're still inside here somewhere."

Evans nodded, picked up a vidphone.

"We'll find them," gasped Steratt, a hand to his bloodied face. "I swear we'll find them!"

Gant looked at him, saying nothing, holding the bodywhip loosely in his hand.

"Here . . . lower him," said Mary-Mary. "Ease him down."

Jessica and the girl slid Logan's body onto a yielding bed of sand, draped with throwcovers, then slipped down beside him, exhausted. Their journey into the mountain's interior had totally sapped their strength. Logan had tried to walk, but his body refused to cooperate; he was a dragging weight between them, an object to be moved through the dark skein of labyrinthine passages, guided only by Mary-Mary's knowledge of the intricate caverns.

They'd reached the cave which was home to the girl. Sunlight shafting down from a high crack in the outer rockface of Crazy Horse provided illumination. It was now mid-afternoon.

Jessica lay in the patch of gold, soaking up the rays, face raised to the welcome yellow warmth. Tears formed in her eyes, rolled down the slope of her cheeks, but she was smiling. "So *long* . . . since . . . I've felt the sun."

"I've been preparing things," said Mary-Mary. "Taking what I knew we'd be needing from Gant's supplies. A little here, a little there." She nodded toward the rear of the cave. "We have food, water, medicine for Logan . . . Even these!" And she folded back a throwcover, revealing two Fusers.

Jessica looked at her. "Gant was going to kill us."

"I know," said the girl. "I've been watching everything. He enjoys inflicting pain. He always did. As a Sandman, he never worried about who got hurt on a hunt. He'd Gun anyone in his way. Homered a seven-year-old once."

"How did you get here—to Crazy Horse?"

"I came with Ballard as part of his Sanctuary Line. When he died I hid in the caverns, stealing the food I needed. They never missed it. I was careful about that."

"Then Gant doesn't know you're alive?"

"No one knows I'm here in the mountain. That's why I've been able to watch, find out what Gant's planning. And it's monstrous."

"I know he's reactivated the Central Core," said Jessica. "But, beyond that—"

"Gant plans to revive the Thinker—use it to bring the cities back to life. If that happens, he'll control the world."

"But Ballard killed the Thinker."

"Not really," said Mary-Mary. "He didn't have enough time. Gant's men were on the way to Crazy Horse when he got there just ahead of them. Ballard did what he could—shorted out the Central Core, destroyed all of the main relays . . . enough to knock out the cities. But Gant homered him before he could effectively destroy the main computer body. The Thinker isn't dead, it's just *sleeping*. And Gant intends to awaken it."

"Can't *find* them! And why not?" Steratt raged at his men. "They're here in the mountain, aren't they? Every exit is sealed. Why haven't you found them?"

"You've got ten thousand caves in there," said the leader of the main-thrust search group. "It would take years to probe all of them. There's just no way to do it. We searched the nearest caverns, but they've gone in deep. Too deep for us to follow."

"What about footprints?"

"Much of the ground is hard rock and shale," said the leader. "We didn't find any footprints."

"Then we'll starve them out," said Steratt. "Time is on our side. Have a double guard assigned to all food and water supply areas. They can't escape the mountain. And when they finally come out we'll be waiting for them."

Logan slept. Mary-Mary had provided clothing for him, had tended the wounds on his body, had fed him. The injections she gave him allowed his body to relax, and begin to restore itself. His natural strength came into play; his muscle tone improved, his skin took on color again.

Sometimes he would awaken, groggy and blinking, on the sandy floor of the cave, crying out Jessica's name. She was always there to hold him, gentle him back to sleep, telling him that they were safe . . . safe . . . safe.

Periodically, Mary-Mary would reconnoiter, then return to the cave with news of Gant's operation.

Jessica had many questions for her: "How does he get people to work for him? Surely he doesn't reward them?"

"Reward them!" Mary-Mary laughed. "Gant buys them on the Market as slave workers. Has them brought here. They work in twenty-four-hour shifts. He has well over a hundred men and women now, keeps them locked in cell units between shifts. Here . . ."

And she sketched a rough map of Gant's headquarters on the floor of the cave. "This building is for the technicians."

"How many of those?"

"Dozens. Computer experts, most of them. They supervise the workers. The key scientist is named Fennister. A real genius. He can restore the Thinker to full performance."

"But why would a man of such brilliance work for Gant?"

"You saw what Gant did to Logan. He uses torture to gain his ends. Fennister knows he'll be tortured to death, slowly, if he fails to do what Gant asks. All of them know that."

"And they all . . . accept this?"

"At first three of the techs rebelled, refused to be a part of Gant's plan. So he used them as examples for the others. What he did to them was . . . terrible to see. Now no one defies Gant. No one."

"Then how can he be stopped?"

Mary-Mary sighed; her eyes darkened. "I don't think he *can* be stopped," she said.

## FENNISTER

Sparks showered and burst blue against the terminal. Fennister 2 thinned the blade of cutting fire from the nozzle of the Flamer and finished the separation, then fused the tri-relay segment. He tested the cable. Perfect.

"Gant's here," said a voice at his elbow. Fennister acknowledged with a nod, wearily putting aside the Flamer and peeling his workgoggles. He was a man ready for Sleep when the cities died, which made him twenty-seven now. He would never have become a runner. It was not in Fennister's nature to duck and dodge and hide and outwit. His world was computer science, and if the Thinker had told him to die he would have quietly obeyed its command and gone willingly to a Sleepshop.

But with the death of the cities he quickly came to realize that life beyond the dictates of a machine was precious. Freed from the duties of computer maintainence, he had met a woman, Lisa 18, and had come to care greatly for her. They'd agreed to have children, planned for the future as pair-bound lovers.

Then outlanders hit them. Lisa had been sold on the Market, and he'd been shipped to Crazy Horse as a worker for Gant. "Supervise the rebirth of the Thinker and I'll see that Lisa is yours," Gant had promised him. "Fail to get this job done and you'll never see her again." Thus, despite strong personal misgivings about the project, he had agreed to head it for Gant.

The Central Core was first—and now it was almost totally restored. The main computer-body would follow, each operation done in the thorough, meticulous fashion that characterized Fennister's work.

But not fast enough to suit Gant. Three of Fennister's best men had been tortured in the past week, another killed outright, and now Gant was coming here again, to the Core, to make fresh demands of his team.

He would not resist these demands; it was not in Fennister's nature to do so. Yet he hated Gant with the same quiet, deep intensity that he brought to his work. To rebuild the Thinker under this man's rule was an agony to Fennister that lived within him each moment of the day and night like the breath in his body.

Gant faced him, his tall shadow falling across Fennister's lean body. As usual, Evans 9 was with him, a devil's duo. The thought bitterly amused Fennister. No one had believed in devils for almost two hundred years, yet Gant and his Sandman-chief were surely prime candidates for demonhood.

"How much longer?" Gant demanded.

"The Core will be a hundred per cent operational within twelve hours. After that, the main body work should take another week to ten days."

Gant fingered the ruby at his throat, turned to Evans. "Tell me what he just said."

"Core to be a hundred per cent within six hours. Main body completed in another three days."

"Impossible!" protested Fennister. "I don't have the technicians . . . the equipment . . ."

"Ah, but you do," said Gant smoothly, giving Fennister a jeweled smile. "We just picked up a dozen more techs for you on the Market. And additional equipment arrives by paravane tonight. You'll meet my schedule . . ." Softly. "Won't you?"

Fennister sighed, tightening his thin lips. "Yes, I'll meet your schedule."

## RECOVERY

A shape, hovering. Hazy, double-imaged. Coming into focus.

A face. A woman's face. Close to his. Smiling.

*Jessica!*

Speechless, tears in his eyes, he held her, sought her lips with his, inhaled the sweet fragrance of her skin, touched at the soft flow of her hair. His arms closed around her convulsively.

"It's all right, Logan," she said to him. "You're safe . . . alive . . . with me. Everything's all *right* now."

He drew in a long, shuddering breath; his eyes never left hers. "I thought I'd lost you forever . . . When the outlanders . . ."

She stopped his words with a finger at his lips. "That's all over—and we're together again."

Logan stood up, swaying, still weak from the effects of the tranquilizing drugs. He looked around him at the cave.

"Where are we? The last thing was . . . the storm."

"We're with Mary-Mary inside Crazy Horse. She saved your life, got us both out of prison, gave you medicine . . ."

Mary-Mary moved up to Logan, took his hands in hers. "I was the little girl in Cathedral," she said. "When you were running."

"I remember," said Logan.

She told him about hiding inside the mountain, unable to go for help . . . about the ominous growth of Gant's force ("He must have fifty Sandmen with him!"). And, finally, about Gant's plan to reactivate the Thinker.

"We've got to stop him," said Logan. "If we don't, he'll start the whole inhuman process again . . . something even worse than death at twenty-one . . . a slow, enslaved death inside the cities. He's got to be stopped before that can happen."

"But how?" asked Mary-Mary. "One man and two women against his armed Sandmen?"

"We'll need help," Logan admitted.

"And who's going to help us?" said Jessica. "The Wilderness People—leaderless since Jonath was killed? . . . They're weak, Logan, vulnerable. Gant would slaughter them in an instant! And how would we get word to them? The mountain is sealed. We can't get out."

"She's right," said Mary-Mary. "Besides, Gant's operation is nearly complete. We've no time to bring in outside help—even if we could find any."

A muscle tightened along Logan's jaw; his eyes were set, intense, fixed on an inner goal. "Then . . . that leaves it to us," he said.

## EAGLE

On Argos, in an ancient book, Logan had once read a short bit of verse, still remembered:

> If you wish
> To enter
> The nest of an eagle,
> You must wear
> His feathers.

Which is why he asked Mary-Mary to take him to the place of workers' supply.

They crouched in cavern gloom, watching the guards.

"Four of them," whispered Logan. "Why four?"

"Gant has doubled the guards on every door," she told him.

Too many, Logan told himself. The doors were useless.

"The roof—is it wired?"

"No," she said.

"Then I'll use that," said Logan, stuffing a Fuser into his belt.

"They'll hear you!"

"Who can hear a cat?" Logan smiled.

And was gone.

On the roof, Logan kept low, moving in a half-run across the flat gray surface. As a Sandman, he'd done this sort of thing many times—entered buildings through stealth. This one would be simple.

He found a ventpipe, leading down, pried loose its cover with the barrel of his weapon, working fast and without sound. Once inside the pipe, he carefully lifted the cover back into place. If anyone checked the roof all would be in order.

A sense of adventure possessed him. He had his strength back, or most of it; he had Jessica, alive and loving him; he had his hatred of Gant to fire the blood in his body. It seemed to Logan, at this moment, that he could not fail, that he was truly invincible. He smiled at the madness of it, but logic did not matter; emotion ruled him, carried him swiftly forward in his plan.

He located the clothing supply room without difficulty. It was precisely where Mary-Mary said it would be. The doorlock was an easy matter, and he slipped inside.

No one on duty. A large room with long steel shelves holding neatly-folded workclothes. Logan selected three bodysuits all in matching blue, and quickly added the same number of gogglemasks and gloves. In removing the items, Logan did as Mary-Mary had done previously with foodstuffs and medical supplies: rearranged the stacks to disguise the fact that anything had been taken.

With what he needed compactly bundled under one arm, Logan glided for the roof. When he heard voices he did not move. When they had faded he resumed. No problems.

Invincible.

They suited up. Masks. Gloves. Bodysuits.

In these dark blue outfits it would be impossible to recognize them. They would blend in perfectly with the other workers, be able to move freely without fear of detection.

When he had conceived the plan Logan intended going alone, but Mary-Mary told him that he'd need her to pinpoint the proper areas. "All right, then, the two of us." No, not good enough. What they had to do required teamwork, and *all* three of them would be needed to get the job done.

Reluctantly, Logan had agreed.

## CORE

The Central Core was Fennister's pride. Working day and night, almost without sleep, toiling in the depths of the Core shoulder-to-shoulder with his men, he had converted a charred, heat-twisted mass of computer metal into its original machined perfection; he had reconstituted the heart of the Thinker. Now that great heart was beating strongly once again, sending its message of power out along mile upon mile of linked cable to all the dark areas of the multi-banked computer.

Life was flowing back into the Thinker.

The Core presently required only a standby crew; the main thrust of Fennister's efforts concerned the vast computer-body itself. He was working desperately to meet Gant's schedule—realizing that it was barely possible to succeed. He *had* to succeed, for the sake of his men, and for Lisa.

Failure was unthinkable.

Three figures detached from cavern shadow . . . three blue-clad workers blending with more than a dozen other blue-clad workers . . . moving toward the Core . . . wearing the full-face gogglemasks required for this high-body-risk area.

The Sandman accompanying this shift-replacement crew noticed nothing unusual; he had not counted the workers. That wasn't his responsibility; if they sent him a dozen or two dozen his job was to guard them at the Core, make sure everything ran smoothly down there. Fennister knew what they should do; he didn't. And didn't give a damn in the bargain. They were sheep to be herded, and he was a bored shepherd.

In the group, Logan kept Mary-Mary and Jessica close to him. Behind the opaque goggles, his eyes raked the area. They were entering the Core itself now, their transbelt taking them down to the glowing, pulsing interior.

"Right on time," said the guard below, his voice muted by the gogglemask he wore.

"When have I ever been late?" growled the Sandman leading Logan's group.

"Have a good shift," said the guard as his early-hours workmen shuffled tiredly onto the return belt.

We made it! Logan exalted. We're here!

With Mary-Mary and Jessica, he moved to a tool-cab just out of the guard's view. Shielding the move with his body, Logan took a needle-thin length of steel from his suit, worked it deftly into the drawerlock. The drawer slid back.

Quickly, each of them removed a Flamer from the inside toolrack. The drawer was closed, locked again.

They moved off.

Logan wasn't sure of his direction. "Which way?" he asked Mary-Mary, his goggled head close to hers.

"I'll lead," she said. "Follow me."

Logan and Jessica stayed close as she weaved a path around giant columns, past glowing relay units, deep into the humming depths of the inner Core.

Now they were totally separated from the other workers, free to implement Logan's plan. The Sandman on duty was long out of sight.

"Is this the right cluster?" asked Logan, pausing before a tangle of multi-colored power cables protruding from the Core's vitals like immense snakes.

"Yes," said Mary-Mary.

Logan knelt to examine them. "If we cut through these and cross-connect them the power overload will blow the Core."

"But how will we get out?" asked Jessica, alarm in her muffled words.

"We'll have some time before the cross-connection takes full effect," Logan told her. "It won't happen all at once. There's only one Sandman on guard, and I can deal with him. We'll be safe inside the caverns by the time it blows."

"Will this really stop Gant?"

"Not completely," said Logan. "But he'll have to rebuild the entire Central Core again. By then we can figure a way out of the mountain and bring help back to fight him. This *will* work, I'm sure of it!"

They each set their Flamers for maximum penetration. Using the high-intensity fire tools, they could slice through the massive cables with relative ease.

But it would be dangerous.

Keen concentration was a necessity; the depth of each cut had to be precise. Too shallow, and the cross-connection could not be achieved; too deep, and the cables would fuse, killing them instantly but leaving the Core intact.

"Ready?" Logan's Flamer was poised in his gloved hand, flickering blue at its tip.

The two women nodded.

"Begin," he said.

And three bright blades of flame began probing at the cables.

## ATTENTION!

Gant was drunk.

He seldom allowed himself the luxury of heavy drinking, but this was a special day of celebration: the Core was fully operational and work was progressing smoothly on the main body of the Thinker. Soon he would be in a position to program it to fit his desires, to light the cities like so many stars in the heavens—and with him in charge of the universe!

Indeed, a day to celebrate.

He'd been drinking Spanish wine with Evans, who was now equally drunk; they blared out songs together in off-key, grunting voices, pounded the table with their fists, roared with laughter at non-existent jokes.

Steratt appeared in the doorway, looking disturbed.

They paid him no heed. He moved to Gant, scowling. "You'd better listen to me," he said.

Drunk or sober, Gant was anything but a fool—and the look in Steratt's eyes told him to listen.

"Did Fennister authorize Flamer use at the Core?" asked Steratt.

"Of course not," snapped Gant. "The Core's done."

"The guard there just checked the tooldrawer. Three Flamers are missing."

Gant's face darkened; his eyes became hooded. The effects of the wine flushed away in the heat of his anger.

"Let's get down there!" he said to Evans.

Logan's cable was neatly severed, ready for re-connection. He watched tensely as Jessica and Mary-Mary bent to their work, flamepoints eating steadily through the tough cable fiber.

Almost finished.

Then; the guard's voice: "What are you three doing?"

Logan knew that bluff would accomplish nothing at this moment. Words were no good at all.

He turned toward the Sandman, triggered the Flamer in his gloved hand. The killing blade of fire caught the guard at shoulder level, knifing through vein and tendon . . .

He spun, gasped, and died.

"Come on!" said Logan. "Move out! Fast!"

"We can *finish,* Logan!" cried Mary-Mary. "Another minute or two. We're nearly—"

He grabbed her arm, propelling her forward. "Suspected something. Wouldn't have come here if he didn't. Probably checked the tools. There'll be others coming."

Isolation was death, Logan knew. Separated and running, they would be spotted easily and trapped in the Core. Protective coloration was their only hope—the eagle's feathers! In gogglemasks and bodysuits all workers were identical; to escape they had to intermix with the other blue-clad figures, then wait their chance to fade back into the caverns.

By the time Logan found the main group Mary-Mary was gone. He turned to Jessica, his tone harsh, demanding: "Where *is* she?"

"She went back—into the Core," said Jessica. "Said she was sure she could finish."

"That's impossible now!" He looked around him. The workers were doing their routine jobs, unaware of the guard's death.

"Stay here," ordered Logan. "I'm going after her. As soon as I—"

"Attention! All workers, attention!" a speakerbox blared. "There has been an accident at the Core. Please use the interior belt and form on Level 6 for inspection."

"Too late," Logan whispered to Jessica, looking toward the upper level. Gant and Evans were there, Steratt beside them.

As the workers reached the top, masks were peeled away, features and IDs scanned.

"We can't go up," said Logan.

"But we can't stay here either," she said.

"Move along, you two." A Sandman prodded them toward the belt.

Logan drove a fist into the man's face, grabbed Jessica's hand, ducking between two central-power columns.

A laser blast sizzled the floor behind them. Gant was shouting, gesturing wildly.

Logan had a goal: an emergency riser used by repair crews he'd seen on the far side of the Core. If they could reach it without being cut off . . .

If.

At the cables, working with the Flamer, Mary-Mary had ignored the demands of the speakerbox, but she could not ignore the shouts, the crackle of laser fire . . .

No chance to finish now. Only a chance to escape.

She threw the Flamer aside, began running toward

the Auxiliary Powerchamber; a stepway there could lift her out of the main danger area.

A black shape filled her vision. A pair of strong arms gripped her; a Gun was jammed against her neck, forcing her head back, painfully.

Sandmen! Two of them, prowling the inner Core.

Instantly, she relaxed, knowing that struggle was useless. She did not resist as the gogglemask was peeled from her face.

"I don't know this one," the first Sandman said.

"She's no worker," said the second.

"I know her," said a harsh, familiar voice.

Mary-Mary drew in a quick, strangled breath—a sob of utter defeat . . .

As her eyes locked on the cruel face of Gant.

## BOLDNESS

"It was my fault," said Logan. "The whole thing, *my* fault."

They'd regained the caverns, had reached the cave of Mary-Mary. Finding it empty, Logan knew at once that the girl had been taken; otherwise, she would have been here, waiting for them.

"But she *insisted* on going back . . . There was no stopping her," said Jessica.

"Not that," said Logan, shaking his head. "I mean the whole plan. It had no chance from the beginning."

"But you're wrong, Logan! It almost worked."

"A thing works or it doesn't. There are no 'almosts,' " he said bitterly. "It was a fool's idea, and it's cost us Mary-Mary."

He slumped to the sandy floor of the cave, eyes dulled with pain in thinking about the girl.

"What will Gant . . . *do* to her?" asked Jessica, easing down beside him. Her voice was soft, the words strained.

"I know him," said Logan tightly. "I know how his mind works. There's no doubt of what he'll do to her."

A long moment of silence. Then Logan quietly said a word. It stiffened Jessica's back; she felt a chill mount her skin as she heard it:

"Stormroom."

Standing naked and alone in the steel chamber, facing the vented walls, Mary-Mary knew she would never leave this place alive. Gant would have his full revenge on her for snatching Logan from his grasp; he would eliminate her with the same terrible device he had used to subdue Logan.

*This* time the storm would continue, would end only when her life ended. She would be battered and destroyed by its hurricane force . . .

Mary-Mary discovered, amazingly, that she was not afraid of death. She had a burning faith in Logan; she knew that, somehow, he'd find a way to stop Gant. No other Sandman had defied the full might of DS, but Logan had done so, and survived. No other Sandman had reached Sanctuary, but Logan had reached it. He was capable of incredible actions, extraordinary deeds—which was why Gant so desperately wanted him dead.

Gant feared Logan 3 as he feared no other man.

Thus, in a deep sense, she was content. Everything she could do had been done. She had revealed Gant's plan to Logan, made him aware of the danger, fired his will and given him a purpose.

He would fulfill that purpose.

Mary-Mary was ready to die.

She felt a stirring in the room. Faintly, imperceptibly, from the wall vents, a soft current of air probed at her.

Mary-Mary shivered.

The storm had begun.

Logan fought the rage that was consuming him. It required a full exertion of will for him to remain a reasoning, thinking man and not a beast bent on slaughter. He fought against an overwhelming impulse to plunge out of the caverns, Fuser in hand, and blast his way to Gant.

I'd never reach him, Logan told himself; they'd burn me down before I was ten steps into the light. Every Sandman in Crazy Horse envisions me dead under his Gun; that sight lives behind their eyes. Gant's reward for my death must, by now, be very great indeed.

Yet he could not hide like a frightened mole in these caves while Gant destroyed the girl who'd saved his life, who'd brought him Jessica . . .

The man, not the beast, would go forth.

But go forth he must!

They were on a thick shelf of rock with a clear view of the large, circular structure just ahead.

Without Mary-Mary, Logan was dependent on Jessica's limited knowledge of Gant's mountain stronghold.

"And you're certain that's it?"

"Yes," said Jessica. "Gant keeps them all locked up there between work shifts."

"Communications?"

"There's a vidphone connecting the prison area directly to Gant's personal quarters."

"Good," nodded Logan. "Who's in charge of the cells?"

"Steratt. You saw him leave."

"How many Sandmen are usually in there?"

"Three. One just inside the door. One patroling the cellblock. Another on the vid-deck. There may be more now."

"I doubt that Gant would use extra men here," said Logan. "This is the *last* place he'd expect me to be."

She looked hard into his eyes; her own were glistening. "Just remember that I love you," she said softly.

"You think I'll never come out . . . That we won't—"

"I love you," she repeated.

And he kissed her.

Boldness was Logan's last hope. No cat-stalking, no stealthy penetration. No time for subtle moves now. Bold action remained to him, and that alone.

He reached the outer door as Jessica melted back into the shadows. With the butt of his Fuser he banged loudly on the metal.

A Sandman's sharp voice from inside: "Who is it?"

"Who do you *think* it is? It's me, Steratt! Open the damn door. My key's with Gant."

Logan held his breath, the Fuser poised in his hand. He had heard Steratt's voice many times from the caverns, and his imitation was convincing. Muffled by the double thickness of the metal door, it might pass.

His heart jumped; the door was opening.

In the flicker of an eye Logan had the guard by the throat. A quick snap—and his head rolled loosely. Logan allowed the body to spill out along the floor as he pulled closed the massive, self-locking door.

He quickly stripped the body, putting on the guard's gray uniform. He pulled the cap low over his eyes, walked casually toward the cellblock.

Twenty feet . . . fifteen feet . . . ten . . .

"I thought Steratt was coming with you," said the second guard, peering down at Logan from his station on the block.

"I come alone," said Logan—and fired straight up at the man.

He didn't wait to see him die; he spun like a dancer in the direction of the vid-deck, leveled his weapon at the third Sandman. Logan's voice cracked across the chamber: "Gun on the deck! Quick!"

Logan could hear the murmur of excited voices from the cells lining the block.

"What's happened?"

"I don't know!"

"Guard's been killed!"

"Who? Who did it?"

"Must be Logan!"

"Logan's here!"

The name ran the cells like a chant: Logan . . . Logan . . . Logan . . .

He was on the vid-deck now, his weapon covering the guard. "Give me the block keys."

"Can't," said the man. His face was pearled with fear-sweat as he looked at the death in Logan's hand.

"Why can't you?"

"Cells are set to open automatically at shift-time, when the crews are changed. Only Gant can open them between shifts."

"Then get him on the vid." Logan's eyes were blood-fired. "Call him over."

"He won't come," protested the guard. "What can I tell him?"

"Tell him you have word of Logan—that you think you know where to find me, but that you want to lead him there yourself, alone, so that no one else can claim the reward."

"He'll never believe that! And if he did he'd bring a dozen men!"

"Your life *depends* on what he believes," said Logan. "He wants me dead by *his* hand. That's Gant's prime passion . . . He'll *want* to believe what you tell him. And personal greed is a thing he understands. He'll come."

The guard, still sweating, turned to the vidphone.

## FLAMER

Gant keyed the outer door, stepped quickly inside.

His step was light. There was an exultation in him. Somehow, this fool guard had discovered Logan's hiding place; the *how* of it didn't matter. No one would come up with such a story unless it were true. What could it gain the man to lie? No one lied to Gant about Logan; no one would be mad enough to try.

It was true, then: Logan 3 was once again within his grasp. And this time nothing on Earth could keep Gant from killing him.

He felt like singing!

But *wait* . . .

He stopped, eyes narrowed. Where was the inner guard? Gant swept his gaze to the upper cellblock.

No guard there either.

A trap!

"You wanted me. I'm here," said a voice from the shadows.

And Logan stepped into the light, a Fuser aimed at Gant's head.

The dark man could not speak; his throat muscles worked convulsively in the shock of this meeting.

"Your Gun . . . let it fall," said Logan.

Gant hesitated, glancing toward the vid-deck.

"No guards to help. They're all dead. *Do* it."

The holstered Gun thumped the floor.

"Now—the central block key. Give it to me."

"I don't have it."

"I won't ask twice." Logan raked the side of Gant's head with the Fuser's barrel. Blood pulsed on the tall man's ripped cheek. He handed over the key.

"All right," said Logan, "walk ahead of me. Fast."

They moved toward the block.

Behind Gant, Logan said, "What have you done with Mary-Mary?"

"She's alive."

"Where?"

"In a cell. Main building."

"She's in the stormroom, isn't she?"

Gant said nothing.

"After I free the workers we're going there. If she's dead you'll wish *you* were . . . and you'll be a long time dying."

After his call to Gant the guard had jumped Logan. A foolish move. But, in killing him, Logan's shot had severed the vid-line. Meaning that there was no way to force Gant to cancel the storm that must, even now, be battering Mary-Mary.

The thought of the girl's anguish distracted Logan for the split-second it took Gant to feint left and kick the Fuser from his enemy's hand.

Logan surged at Gant. But, like a great dark cat, the man had whipped back—to palm a wall switch.

Instantly, a series of mirror-bright steeloid panels dropped from above, sealing Logan within a circular area perhaps thirty feet across. A final panel slid over the others to form a dome above his head.

Leaving him blind and alone.

Outside, the triumphant voice of Gant: "Another of my inventions, Logan . . . in case I had to discipline one of my workers. And really quite imaginative . . . *Watch!*"

The blackness grew less intense as the circular walls surrounding Logan began to glow. Heat began to sweat Logan's skin; the panels glowed a furious blue-orange. The heat was stifling.

This place was an oven—an immense human cookery, in which Gant literally *roasted* his victims!

Logan bellied flat, knowing the heat would rise, giving him a partial respite from the worst of it. But his gesture was futile. Each breath he took scalded his lungs. His eyes burned. He'd be dead soon enough, his flesh blistered and curled to ash.

Gant's final revenge.

Logan's thoughts reeled in confusion: the heat seemed to be *lessening,* not increasing!

The glow slowly faded from the walls. Darkness returned.

And with it, the voice of Gant: "You didn't think I'd let you die in there, did you, Logan? And cheat myself of watching your finish? No, that would never do. Not after all we've been through together."

What was next? What new torture had Gant devised?

"I'm coming in, Logan. To watch you die. But under *my* hand. I don't want one of my inventions to finish you. That pleasure I reserve for myself."

And a panel slid back. Light flooded the circular area.

Logan squinted, saw Gant standing with a Flamer in his jeweled hand.

"You were using one of these in your clumsy attempt to destroy my beautiful Core. Now it's only appropriate that I use it to destroy you."

And the panel whispered shut, killing the light.

Logan and Gant were together in darkness.

## DUEL

On the rock shelf, Jessica waited.

Logan had told her he would need her help if he managed to free the workers. Until then, all she could do was await some sign of his success.

It did not come.

She'd seen Gant enter the prisoners' compound alone, and assumed that Logan was responsible for his appearance—but no one had come out. Not Logan. Not Gant. Not the workers.

What had happened inside the compound?

Logan knew that the first rule of fighting in the dark is not to be where your enemy *expects* you to be. Therefore, as the steel panel was sliding closed, killing the light, Logan was in swift motion, catapulting himself across ten feet of flooring.

A long bloom of yellow-green flame told him he'd been correct—as Gant aimed at the spot where Logan had been standing. The fire lit the chamber for a brief instant, showing Gant Logan's new position.

Again, he triggered the Flamer.

And, again, Logan was gone.

A dry chuckle from the darkness. "I could make this an easy kill," Gant's voice declared. "In one hand, the Flamer, in the other a flashbeam. To pick you out, Logan. To reveal you in the dark . . ." The chuckle was repeated. "But that would be too simple. There would be no joy in it. I want our little . . . contest to last. I want to *enjoy* burning you to ash."

In one way, Gant was wrong. Even with a flashbeam, spotting Logan's exact position within the circle would be difficult—since the polished curving-steel panels acted like a hundred mirrors, casting back a multiplicity of images in their reflective surfaces.

If Logan kept moving . . .

His foot caught on a panel projection; he stumbled. Instantly, a blade of flame jabbed at him. He rolled away from the heat blast, his right leg singed, the cloth burnt away to raw skin.

"Close, eh, Logan?" the taunting voice asked him. "Since I've been reworking the Thinker I've become quite adept in the use of a Flamer. As you are discovering!"

The voice never came from the same spot of darkness long enough for Logan to get a fix on it. Gant knew he'd come for him if he had a stationary target. So each man kept circling, kept fluid . . . wary, alert . . .

Logan was weaponless. Just his bare hands against the kill-power of a Flamer. Gant had called this a contest. No contest; an *execution.*

Then Logan realized Gant had stopped moving.

Logan froze, locking his muscles, stopping the breath in his lungs.

Gant was motionless, listening.

Logan, too. Motionless.

Can he hear the pounding of my heart? Logan wondered. It sounded, within his body, as loud as a hammered drum.

The silence grew, became intolerable.

Logan's mouth was dry; he wanted desperately to swallow—but the faint sound would draw Gant's fire as surely as a shouted word.

His right leg was aching terribly; the flesh, from thigh to ankle, throbbed with stinging pain. Logan *had* to shift the leg, ease it. Didn't want to. Shouldn't. But . . .

Had to.

Gant fired.

Flame ate at Logan, his writhing body mirrored and multiplied a thousand times in the sudden heat-glow.

It had not been a direct hit. Had it been, he'd be dead at this moment. But, instinctively, he'd twisted his torso sideways and rolled with the flame as its cutting edge assaulted him.

From the blackness, Gant roared his delight. "Taste the fire, Logan! Taste its sting! . . . There's no more running for you. No Sanctuary to reach. No Jessica. No Ballard alive to help you . . ."

He was saying more, taunting Logan in a triumphant, mocking voice. Gant began to laugh, and in so doing made one vital mistake: he forgot to keep moving.

Logan had slipped the belt from his tunic, fisting it tight at each end. He launched himself at the sound of Gant's laughter, in a collision of flesh . . .

A shocked, strangled gasp burst from the tall man as Logan's body bore him floorward. The Flamer was knocked, spinning, into darkness.

"Damn you!" cried Gant, his huge hands at Logan's throat.

He had the strength of ten; he was truly a giant, superbly conditioned, a fighting machine of awesome capability—fired with hatred for this tenacious enemy who continued to plague him, who dared, even now, to physically attack him.

He would crush the life from Logan!

*He's killing me! I'm getting dizzy. Mind's blanking. Can't breathe!*

But Logan broke the hold. Using his feet, he snap-kicked free, twisted, looped the narrow belt around the giant's thick neck, applied fierce pressure.

Gant fought him. For a long moment it was impossible to say which man had the greater advantage. Two ex-Sandmen, trained to kill, masters of their craft. Each driven to hate, each determined to end the other's life.

Abruptly, Gant's hands fell away from Logan. He

beat the floor with the flat of his palms—as a panicked bird beats its feathers under the hawk.

The great dark hands went slack; the fingers curled, twitched, fluttered. And did not move again.

Gant was dead.

## ROUT

She saw him!

"Logan!"

"Jess!"

Workers were flooding out of the cells, arming themselves with Flamers, metal clubs, stones . . . rushing toward the door which Logan had opened wide.

"What are you doing *here?*"

"I came to face Gant," she said, trembling, holding him. "When you didn't come out . . . when *no* one came out . . . I thought he'd killed you!"

"It's Gant who died," he told her. "Now do as I said. I'm going after Mary-Mary."

Nodding, she vanished off into a twist of cavern gloom.

Evans 9 got the word first: Breakout. Main block. All the cells emptied.

Where were the guards?

And where was Gant?

No matter. Evans could handle a ragtag band of half-starved workers. He *needed* a bit of excitement; things had been dull since Logan's escape.

He was probably hopelessly lost by now in the caverns, and Jessica with him. Without Mary-Mary they'd have no chance.

Evans was at the vidphone. "Which way are the workers headed?"

The vid gave no reply; the image screen was blank. A malfunction was annoying at a time like this.

Evans strapped on his Gun, stuffed an extra Fuser into his belt, left the unit.

Steratt and the others were outside, battle-assembled, ready to move against the escapees. Evans smiled. His men would grind the rebels underfoot. A mere flexing of Sandman muscle.

It would be amusing.

Logan was at the door of the storm chamber. Through the thick metal walls he could hear the hurricane roaring inside.

"Kill it," he said to the control-tech in front of him, his Fuser jabbing the man's back.

The tech mouthed fear-words, palmed a primary switch on the weatherboard.

The storm died.

"Door," snapped Logan. "Get it open."

The tech did that.

Logan clubbed him aside and vaulted into the room.

She was alive.

"There!" shouted Evans, pointing. "There they are."

Steratt and the Sandmen advanced toward the workers. A narrow stretch of rock tunnel separated the two groups.

The Sandmen moved into the tunnel, Guns ready.

The workers halted, seemed confused. They murmured among themselves.

"The poor fools aren't even firing at us," grinned Steratt. "Maybe they think we'll make it easier on them if they give up now."

"Too bad," sighed Evans, his Gun raised. "I was actually looking forward to—"

He didn't finish.

Evans and Steratt and the entire group of advancing Sandmen were buried in a sudden, crushing downfall of rock . . . huge boulders loosed in deadly profusion by willing hands from above.

Under the personal direction of Jessica 6.

The tunnel was still.

Not a shot had been fired, yet the battle had been won.

## COUNTDOWN

Fennister simply could not believe it, could not accept the fact that it had all happened so quickly, that one man and one woman had routed Gant's army, had freed the workers and turned his universe upside down.

"My whole reason for existence here, for months, has been to make the Thinker live again," he said to Logan. "And now you want me to let it die?"

"No," said Logan, "not *let* it die. I want you to destroy it. Totally. So it can't be revived again, by anyone. No more rule-by-computer. Ever."

"But with Gant dead . . . you and I . . . we could *use* it, for the good of man, not his enslavement."

"There's no good in it," said Logan.

Fennister shook his head.

"And if there was," Logan continued, "who's to say how long we'd control it? Every power-hungry maniac in the world would be licking his chops over the thought of running it. No, Fennister, the Thinker has to die."

They were in the scientist's lab, beyond the inner Core, a vast place of complex instrumentation, filled with a dazzling array of multi-operational equipment which Gant had supplied.

Nothing had been stinted here.

Jessica stood beside Logan; she shared his passion. Fennister's argument made no dent in their combined determination to destroy the source of so much pain and death in the world they'd known.

"We'll finish the job Ballard started," said Logan.

Fennister nodded slowly. "All right . . . we can do it. But the whole mountain must go with it. That's the only way."

Logan was shaken by this. To bring down the great warrior who symbolized courage and rebellion, who ruled the Dakota wilderness in proud granite majesty . . .

But he hesitated for only a moment. His eyes were hard. "The mountain, then," he said.

It would be difficult—and dangerous.

A timing device was set to detonate thermo charges planted at a multitude of spots inside the caverns. For days, Fennister and his technicians had labored to plant these charges and regulate them, precisely, to the primary timer; each had a separate and vital function.

"I want everyone clear of the mountain before we set the timer," said Logan.

"Someone will have to remain in the laboratory," said Fennister. His face was drawn with exhaustion, his eyes pouched and swollen from lack of sleep.

"Why?"

"To make certain the device works. There's no way to monitor it from outside."

"What's the risk factor?" asked Logan.

"It could be high. There's a chance I won't come out."

"You?"

"Who else would it be?" Fennister said in a calm, weary tone. "I'm the only one qualified to see that the timer functions properly."

"I'll do it," said Logan flatly. "Just tell me what I need to know."

Fennister tapped his head. "It's all in here, Logan. And only *I* have it." He spread his hands. "There's no one else."

A moment of silence.

"You'd die with the Thinker?"

"If I must."

Logan was silent for a moment.

"Let's get started," he said.

The Dakota sun was a disc of white gold in the heated morning sky. Under it, well back from the mountain, surrounded by green pines and thick, waist-high brush, the workers and technicians of Crazy Horse stood nervously.

They said nothing; their eyes were on the mountain, fixed to the immense granite figure who seemed tall enough to rule the world.

Jessica stood close to Logan, gripping his hand. Her eyes, too, were on the mountain. Near them, Mary-Mary, pale from her experience in the storm-room, but sharing their joy in having aborted Gant's plan.

"How much longer?" Mary-Mary asked.

"Fennister set the timer exactly," said Logan. "At his signal, we're to count down from a hundred. By the count of twenty-five he should be back here with us."

"He's a brave man," said Jessica.

Logan nodded. "And a brilliant one. The world *needs* its Fennisters now."

"Will he make it?" asked Mary-Mary.

Logan looked at the cavern entrance, a dark wound in the base of Crazy Horse.

"I don't know," he said.

The signal was given.

And the countdown began.

## EXTINCTION

A muted, murmurous sea of voices, counting down to zero, each voice strained, tight with emotion . . .

". . . eighty-two . . . eighty-one . . . eighty . . . seventy-nine . . ."

All eyes on the mountain.

Logan and Jessica and Mary-Mary counting with the others. ". . . sixty-six . . . sixty-five . . . sixty-four . . ."

As Logan's voice mechanically chanted the countdown, like some terrible litany, his mind kept giving him the image of Fennister, alone at the timer, watching for any flicker of imperfection, any sign that all was not well.

". . . forty-eight . . . forty-seven . . . forty-six . . ."

A maddening vision.

Logan felt himself beginning to tremble. His right leg throbbed, still bearing the mark of Gant's Flamer. When *he* was under pressure, in a highly-dangerous situation, this condition could never have manifested itself—but his fear now was for Fennister. And this fear twisted and ate at Logan.

". . . thirty-eight . . . thirty-seven . . . thirty-six . . ."

*Dammit, he should be coming out by now!*

The dark cavern mouth gaped, silent and empty.

". . . twenty-nine . . . twenty-eight . . ."

"I'm going in to get him," said Logan.

"You're not," said Jessica. It was a flat statement.

"Hold her," Logan said to a worker next to them. "She'll try to follow me."

"Logan, you—"

But he did not hear her voice any longer. Her voice was a million miles behind him.

There was only the mountain.

And Fennister.

The count stood at sixteen when Logan reached the lab.

Fennister was gone!

The timer stood deserted—ticking away life-seconds: fourteen . . . thirteen . . . twelve . . .

Logan shouted, "Fennister!"

"Back here," a voice said from the depths of the laboratory.

Logan found him, kneeling at a terminal, adjusting a tiny set screw, grabbed his arm, jerked him upward.

. . . nine . . . eight . . .

"Out!"

"But there's still a loose connection here. I have to—"

"I said *out!*"

And Logan dragged him toward the lab door.

. . . five . . . four . . . three . . .

Logan stared desperately at the timer. "We're too late! The whole mountain's going!"

"No!" Fennister threw his body across the space between Logan and the timing device.

And killed it.

The timer stopped.

"I didn't intend to come out," admitted Fennister. "Gant was my only chance to find Lisa again. He's dead, so I—"

"We'll *find* her," vowed Logan. "I know the Market now. She'll be found, I swear it."

"I believe you."

"Then destroy the Thinker—and come out with me."

"I can't reset the timer," said Fennister. "It's not possible without detonating the charges."

"Can they be rigged to go off any other way?"

"Yes. By fuse. But that's death for us."

"Are you certain?"

"A short fuse is required. We'd have no time to clear the mountain."

"How much time is no time?" Logan asked him.

"Perhaps . . . fifteen . . . twenty seconds. No more."

"We can make it," said Logan. "Go ahead."

Fennister made the proper connection, attached the short length of fuse.

"No way to ignite it," he said.

Logan pulled the Fuser from his belt. "I'll use this," he said.

They moved to the door, poised to run. "Start," Logan told the scientist. "I'll fire, and follow you."

"But I—"

"Run, damn you!"

Fennister took off, leaving Logan alone.

He aimed carefully—triggered the burnweapon.

The fuse ignited, began running a thin line of orange flame rapidly toward the charges.

Logan tossed the weapon aside and sprinted after Fennister.

And soon caught him. "Faster!" yelled Logan.

They ran.

Along the main corridor.

Through a linking series of rooms.

Down a secondary corridor.

Up a flight of cut-stone steps.

Ahead: the bright mouth of the escape tunnel and, just beyond, the exit into Dakota sun, shining with the promise of life itself.

Fennister stumbled, fell, with a snapping of bone, full-face onto the tunnel's dirt floor.

. . . as the fuse burned closer.

Logan pulled at him. "Up!"

"Broken," gasped Fennister. "Thigh bone. Can't walk. Go on, Logan! There's no time to—"

Logan grappled the scientist's body, slinging Fennister's full weight across his shoulders.

"Keep your arms locked around my chest," he said. "Hang on!"

And he staggered forward.

Mary-Mary cried out Logan's name as she saw the two figures emerge from darkness into light.

Jessica's throat was locked; she could not speak.

Several of the workers ran to Logan and Fennister, bore them swiftly away from the mountain. They cleared it.

Barely.

Inside the lab: a final spark of flame.

Then a blinding radiance.

Concussion!

The mountain screamed—a sound of cracking, rending granite and Tashunca-uitco began to die.

A hairline split appeared in the shoulder of Crazy Horse; the immense arm of the great war chief of the Ogallala Sioux, on which five hundred men could stand shoulder-to-shoulder, suddenly quaked loose, sundering into giant boulders.

The massive head of the warrior split itself in twain, as if a titanic axe-blade had cleaved the skull . . .

The huge stallion, bearing the chief, reared up magnificently, magically alive, as tons of rock folded into an opening crevasse behind it; a raised hoof sheared away, fell into disintegrating fragments . . . The main body of horse and man swayed majestically for a moment, then bowed, tumbling down in an awesome granite rain of rock and rubble and dust . . .

A terrible, mind-numbing silence.

As if the universe itself had been extinguished.

## TOGETHER

Jessica turned her eyes to Logan in the down-sifting dust. Like his, her skin was powdered white. Tears had cut furrows down her cheeks.

They embraced, silently.

Something evil had died with the Thinker. Not the computer itself, but the uses to which men put it; no longer would its machine-metal dictate life and death.

Men like Gant could never use it to enslave a world.

"It's done, Logan," she said. "Really done now."

He held her body tightly to his.

"With Jonath dead," said Jessica, "the Wilderness People will need a new leader . . . They need *you,* Logan."

"No more leading," he said darkly. "That's the wrong word for us. I'll help the People . . . You'll help them . . . Mary-Mary will help . . . Fennister . . . all of us." He framed her face with his hands. "Together!"

And the sun burned, and burned, and burned . . . in the arched sky of the Black Dakotas.

## AUTHOR'S AFTERWORD

The world of Logan and Jessica is a very real one to me. I've lived in it, off and on, since July of 1963, when I created the character of Logan the Sandman.

Logan was quite modest in scope that summer. I had no major plans for him. When I came up with the idea of an over-populated world with a compulsory death-law built into it, and a special police group to enforce this law, I thought of it mainly as a projected short story.

My policeman-protagonist, having reached the death age, would run from his own system, using his unique knowledge of it to escape annihilation. That was really all I had at the time.

Now there are (with this book) two Logan novels, an MGM motion picture, a television series—and a line of Logan comic books. With more ahead.

I owe a debt of gratitude to several people for the expansion of my basic idea into its present mass-media form:

To George Clayton Johnson, who contributed a great deal to the world of Logan and Jessica as co-author of *Logan's Run*, published in 1967.

To George Pal, who was largely responsible for the novel's purchase by MGM in 1968, and who worked hard to bring Logan to the screen. Due to administrative problems at the studio, he was forced to abort the project.

To Saul David, who not only produced the hugely-successful, Oscar-winning film version of *Logan's Run*, but who also served as my co-author on the television pilot script written for MGM/CBS in 1976.

To Sydny Weinberg, my editor at Bantam Books, who helped put together the complex and unusual contract for this sequel novel. She's been a staunch Logan enthusiast from the outset!

To Archie Goodwin, at the helm of Marvel Comics, who guided Logan and Jessica through their illustrated adventures.

To all of these sterling individuals—sincere thanks for helping Logan to live, love and fight in his special world of tomorrow. I intend to keep him running for a long time to come!

William F. Nolan
Woodland Hills, California

1977

## ABOUT THE AUTHOR

William F. Nolan is the author of thirty books, half of which are in the science fiction genre. He also writes mysteries, and was twice awarded the Edgar Allan Poe Special Award from the Mystery Writers of America. His work has appeared in over a hundred publications, ranging from *The Magazine of Fantasy and Science Fiction* to *Playboy*, and he has also been a book and magazine editor. Mr. Nolan has written several television movies, including *The Norliss Tapes, Trilogy of Terror* and *Melvin Purvis, G-Man,* and his screenplays include *Burnt Offerings* and *The Legend of Machine-Gun Kelly*. One of his television films recently won the Golden Medallion, presented at the Fourth International Festival of Science Fiction and Fantasy Films in Paris. His work has been widely translated and selected for numerous "best" anthologies. In addition, Mr. Nolan was recently awarded an honorary doctorate for his lifelong contributions to the field of science fiction by the American River College in Sacramento, California. He lives with his wife, Kam, in Woodland Hills, California.